Practicing Murder

Erin Unger

Practicing Murder
COPYRIGHT 2019 by Erin Unger

Contact Information: titleadmin@pelicanbookgroup.com

Cover Art by *Nicola Martinez*

Harbourlight Books, a division of Pelican Ventures, LLC
www.pelicanbookgroup.com PO Box 1738 *Aztec, NM * 87410

Harbourlight Books sail and mast logo is a trademark of Pelican Ventures, LLC

Publishing History
First Harbourlight Edition, 2019
Paperback Edition ISBN 978-1-5223-0213-1
Electronic Edition ISBN 978-1-5223-0211-7
Published in the United States of America

Dedication

To my husband Mike, who believed I would become a
bona fide author someday, even when I doubted.

1

No amount of hiding at the carnival was going to change what Maddie Clare faced. She clutched a bag of pink cotton candy and bit the last of the caramel apple in her other hand, not really tasting the tart and sweet combination. The apple caught and then slid down her throat as she turned away and swiped at a tear. Maddie scooted past a couple with a stroller who weaved in front of her as they eyed the different games and food vendors along the long strip of carnival booths.

The dusky sky, the music, even the smell of popcorn and funnel cakes wouldn't send her belly into a frenzy of happiness. This was the break she needed, yet it only reminded her even more of her aunt. Her eyes stung. *No, no, please don't start crying again.*

Why couldn't God have let Aunt Lonna live? Why did her commuter plane have to have a landing gear malfunction just shy of the landing strip at the airport?

And here Maddie was once again, back at home with its claws of bad memories. If she could just get through the release of her aunt's body and the funeral, she'd rush back to college and bury herself in finals with her favorite Cheezits in one hand and the comfort of her best wonky pen in the other. Then there'd be no time for the gnawing sadness to bury itself in her belly.

Maddie wiped the moisture off her cheek and then

scanned the thoroughfare for a trashcan. The sky dropped into darkness, fighting with the glaring lights of the rides that dared to reach up and touch it. Was there a garbage can in this place? Had the carnival workers forgotten the clean parks campaign? The town of Anby had spent a decent amount of money enforcing it in the last year. A narrow alley separated a ring toss booth and a neon-painted dart game stand. She spotted a garbage can and bent to avoid the humongous purple unicorn that hung low from a wire of prizes as she walked deep into the makeshift alley. The shadows fought to hide the metal barrel overflowing with half-empty popcorn bags and plates smeared with pizza guts. Music seeped from the ring toss booth, and there was a crescendo in volume as if she'd stepped right up to the speakers that filtered the sound to the whole park.

Maddie raised her hand to gauge the distance to the trashcan and let the apple stick fly through the air. Hopefully, it wouldn't miss and land in the sea of waste on the grass.

Before she turned away, Maddie bumped against something hard. She stiffened. *What?* She hadn't thought there'd been a wall behind her. A millisecond later, all her senses enraged her fight or flight instinct, but a crushing force pulled her arm tight to the side of her body and pinned her.

The cotton candy bag fell to the ground.

Panic spun her into a daze, yet she tried to push away from the large form that held her. Maddie couldn't think. Blood rushed in her ears and her heart pounded. Even the breath in her lungs hissed out like a pressure cooker about to blow as the force that held her squeezed.

She bit against the salty palm smashing her mouth and pulled her jaw to the side with a wrenching force.

A scream echoed in her chest but died before it had air to release.

"You tell anyone and you'll disappear forever." The low whisper of a man's voice streaked across her ear to her cheek, bringing tears to her eyes with the heat of his words.

She tried to shake free. Her heart drummed against her rib cage. Todd? No, please not him. Was she to be at his mercy again? She tried to block the image of his face leering at her as he'd seized her all those years ago. But she'd escaped once. Was he back after all this time?

The man's grip tightened around her neck and stopped all airflow. "Your aunt didn't know what she was talking about. And you're going to keep your mouth shut about what she told you, or I'll make you shut up."

Not Todd. She kicked backward, made contact, and then grabbed his pinkie. Turning her head into his elbow, Maddie tried to suck in a breath and pulled with all her strength on the tiny appendage.

He yelled and tumbled backward, almost pulling her to the ground with him.

Maddie braced her knees and fought the tiny dancing lights that zigzagged at the corners of her vision like lightning bugs flashing their iridescent tails in a stand of trees. Before Maddie could turn, the force of his body throttled her forward once again. Her outstretched hand dropped to the ground as he pushed her toward the metal trashcan.

As if the carnival manager had flipped the power switch to the entire park, the lights in her eyes died in a flash of darkness.

2

Joze Evans pulled his EMT bag close to his chest and rushed past a group of teens in tight jeans and logoed T-shirts, who'd just dumped a load of trash onto the freshly mowed grass. Did they want a one-way ticket out of the park? Because they were going to get it if they dropped one more empty bottle onto the carnival grounds.

He swiveled and pointed at the mess as he took in the pinched face of one particular boy in the center of the clique. Travis, his boss's son. Of course, it would be him causing trouble. There was no time to deal with the delinquents, but he couldn't let the litter violation go. "Travis, please pick up that mess."

All of the teens eyed him with raised brows.

"Now."

A few girls tittered and stared. Travis drew a few inches from him before backing off and taking in his EMT uniform. "What you gonna do about it, Evans? Not like you're a cop or anything."

Of course, the ring leader would have the nerve to push his buttons tonight, even if he was trying to hide an ounce of fear in his squirrelly eyes.

"Have some respect."

Without waiting to see if he obeyed, Joze rushed past them. Where was the kiddy Space Ride? A little girl who'd caught her finger in the release shaft of the seat waited to be checked out. As he moved between two makeshift booths and into a narrow alley, he swung out his EMT bag. Man, trash littered the ground here too. Deep shadows shrouded an overflowing garbage pail that crowded the walkway.

He stumbled over something large and solid and tried to catch his balance before he slid headlong into the refuse. Wait a minute. Was that a body against his shin?

He retracted his booted foot and grabbed his LED flashlight off his belt. Blond hair fell over a woman's face. She moaned.

He knelt and gripped her shoulder. "Ma'am. Ma'am, can you hear me? Hold still."

She started to pull away from the glare of his flashlight.

"Don't move."

"Hu—"

"I said hold still. You could have a neck injury." Joze held her in place. "Do you know what happened?"

She raised a shaky hand to her hair and pushed it out of her face.

The cute nose. The soft jawline. *No.* With all the mental strength he could muster, Joze held his ground. *Please God, not this woman.* He worked his jaw to decrease the pressure that pounded through his ears.

"Madeline." No way was he going to let her keep him from doing his job, even if she was the last woman he wanted to help.

She cracked open dazed eyes. "What— happened?"

When her gaze focused on him, she tried to

wrench out of his grasp.

He grunted. "You need to remain immobile. I don't know the full extent of your injuries." Into the mic at his shoulder, he said, "Jim, I need a stretcher out by the ring toss and dart booths. Woman, twenty-six years of age, is down. Possible neck or head injury. Can you send another EMT to the child with the stuck finger? She's at the Space Ride."

The clear voice on the other end responded, "Sure thing. Be right there."

He was more than aware of the heat radiating from her shoulder and hip into his hands.

Think about the job. This was nothing more than a woman who needed his medical attention. Forget it was the woman who'd walked out on him and tried to ruin his best friend's life.

Maddie pushed his hand off her hip. "Let go of me." Her voice was clearer now. "I didn't injury...I mean injure...my neck...I don't think."

Garbled language. Could be a concussion at the very least.

"I can't, ma'am." He failed to hold back the emphasis on the word "ma'am."

Her eyes opened so wide.

Don't even think of falling into those baby blues.

She clamped her jaw and fought against him until he released her. "What are you doing here?"

"Trying to help you."

"Leave me alone, Joseph Evans."

Had she forgotten how much he hated his given name? She'd probably used it on purpose.

She pushed with a force to rival one of his old wrestling buddies.

Before he could restrain her again, Maddie sat up

and put her hand to her head. Great. Non-compliance. And a woman who could get him in a world of trouble just by opening her mouth. Like before. And knowing Maddie, it would be her goal to do so. Yet there was a twinge in his chest. The red mark on her forehead began to swell as he stared at it. "I know I'm the last person you want to see." *You're the last one I want to be working on.* "But let me do my job and help you."

Her hand flew out and blocked his attempt to palpate her head for other injuries. Was that a stray tear? From Maddie? A tough girl...or at least four years ago she'd never have cried in front of him. He couldn't stop the softer tone that crept into his voice. "It'll only take a minute, and then you'll never see me again."

3

"Joze, back off." The steel edge to Maddie's voice didn't stop him from checking her vertebrae with his nimble fingers. She tried to get her bearings. He was an EMT now?

He pulled back and ran a hand through his black hair. It was longer than he used to keep it. Still straight as an arrow.

Maddie shook off the thought and took in the tomato sauce and buttery-popcorn-scented trash she sat on. What was she doing on the ground? She scooted to the vinyl-walled booth behind her and held her temples. "Am I still at the carnival?"

There wasn't enough space between her and Joze and his inquiring brown-eyed gaze. No distance was far enough. If she'd had the sheer strength, she'd have run to her car and escaped the carnival before he could answer, but her body didn't want to comply.

Another EMT jogged over to Joze, followed by a third, shorter one. The stretcher bounced in between them from the ruts in the grass.

Memories overflowed Maddie's conscience. Arms squeezing her tight. Someone whispered to keep silent.

The two men left the gurney and came closer, but Joze drew back a fraction. "Do you know what happened?"

She eyed him.

The taller EMT looked from Joze to her and back. Had he heard the end of their conversation? Her biting remark and Joze's almost pleading answer?

"I'm Jim. I'll be taking a look at you, OK?" His hand went up as if to ward off Joze. "Go get me the neck brace. I forgot it at the ambulance."

Joze frowned. "I have one in my bag."

The guy pulled Joze aside, but she could still hear their hushed conversation. "Man, I think she needs a little space. You have some history with her?"

He nodded but kept his mouth shut in a thin line. Like the last time she'd seen him.

"We need a minute to evaluate this situation."

"OK." Joze grimaced. He moved away, scratching the back of his neck.

Jim slid on gloves with care, wriggling his sausage-shaped fingers into them as if to keep them from tearing and then lightly examined her head with his fingertips. "You've got a good bump right here. You could have a concussion."

The other EMT shined a light on her forehead. "Any nausea, dizziness?"

Maddie pressed her hand to her overfull stomach. "A little."

With his strong, steady hands, Jim continued to check her over as the other man took her pulse. "Can you remember what happened? Did you fall?"

Maddie blew out a breath. "No. Well, yes. Someone grabbed me from behind and pushed me." Confusion reigned, her brain still addled.

She squeezed her eyes closed and shivered. "I don't know who it was."

He gave the other EMT a sharp glare. "Walk me through what you do remember."

"The guy squeezed me so hard." She laid her head back against the wall with care and tried to concentrate. "I almost managed to get away for a second." She gulped in air. "But I don't know what happened after that. And I don't know who it was."

Joze returned to them, throttling down the small makeshift alley. "Here." He almost threw the brace at his partner, his gaze trained on her. "Figure anything out while I was gone?"

Neither EMT looked at Joze but kept their attention on her.

Maddie pointed at the brace. "I don't need that. See, I can move fine." She bent her head back and forth. "It's my head, that's all." The movement shot pain through her eyes. "Ow." She held up a hand. "Don't worry. Just my head again. I moved too fast."

One of Jim's gloves ripped as he tried to adjust it. He reached in his pocket and pulled out another one. "Joze, call Officer Tuttle. She needs to make a statement, and the scene needs to be secured while we take her to the ambulance. Someone did this to her."

Maddie squeezed her eyes closed to stop the pounding in her head, but she couldn't help glancing in Joze's direction.

His jerky movements made her raise her eyebrows, and he stared at her as he called for the officer.

He looked worried. For her? He wouldn't care about her.

"Did you see your assailant in any way? Maybe his shoes or clothing? Do you recognize anything about him?" Jim interrogated.

"I don't know. He grabbed me from behind." She clutched her chest. Why her? What did the guy mean by what he'd said? She didn't know anything. In fact, she hadn't been home for a long time. If it hadn't been for her aunt's death, she'd still be away at college getting ready to finish up her master's degree in environmental health and safety engineering.

Her body shook. How many years had passed since the last time…She shook off the growing pressure in her chest. *Don't give in to it. Breathe. Don't think right now.*

A police officer entered the alley and got a quick history on the situation from Joze and Jim. Then he turned to her.

Please let this go quick.

"Ma'am, what's your name?"

"Madeline Clare. I go by Maddie." She told him what little she knew. A tremble began in her hand and took over her body. Why wouldn't the shaking stop? Even clutching her hands together didn't settle her nerves.

When she finished, Jim went for the stretcher again.

She shot her hand up. "No. I'm not going to the hospital. I need a minute, that's all."

In unison, the EMTs protested.

"I don't need to."

Joze took a step closer. "You really should let a doctor decide that. You may need a CT scan—"

"I mean it." The nausea began to let up. If only the pounding would stop and the shakiness in her hands would subside.

He squatted in front of her, sending a whiff of his body wash her way. The scent brought back too many memories…of times she'd spent in his arms. *Don't go there.* Maddie shut her eyes and tried to think of anything else.

"Well, can we at least take you to the ambulance to rest for a bit? You can talk more there with Officer Tuttle."

Maddie pushed up to a stand and put her hands out for a moment. The earth tilted. She gulped. It steadied, and she opened her eyes again. Why be dumb and take too many risks? "All right."

Officer Tuttle checked the ground around her and spoke into his mic, calling more officers. "I have a few more questions, but I'll have another officer meet you over there."

Her eyes darted back and forth as Jim held her elbow and they walked. It took all her strength not to lean into Jim.

Joze kept throwing glances her way but maintained his distance. She'd outright dismiss him if she could. Ignoring him for now would have to do.

Maddie shoved her hand into her left pocket. Wait a minute. Where was her wallet? The one Aunt Lonna had given her on her eighteenth birthday. The one she loved even though it was a twelve-year-old's dream with pink owls all over it. A shock wave of apprehension ran through her. "My wallet's gone."

Jim guided her forward. "Joze, can you alert Officer Tuttle?" To her, he said, "They'll look into it. Are you sure you had it at the time of the attack?"

"Yes."

She lifted her chin and begged herself not to watch Joze as he glanced at her before striding back toward the alley.

It wasn't working. Straight, dark hair fell across his forehead. Fine cheekbones. Brown eyes the color of her favorite milk chocolate bar.

She pulled her gaze from him. *Think of anything.* Cold arms squeezing the life out of her jumped to the forefront of her mind. *Not that. Think of anything but that.* But a chill had already set in her bones. And now her attacker had her driver's license, old address, and all.

4

Joze couldn't leave Maddie's side. Not now. She might run her mouth and lie to his buddies like she was so good at doing. He fought the urge to refuse a return to the crime scene. Why did he have to be the one to turn back and talk to the officer? But then he didn't need Jim reporting bad patient relations to his boss, either. He'd better hurry back before she had a chance to spread lies about him like she did about his best friend. Who knew what she'd come up with?

Joze approached Officer Tuttle, who continued to take pictures of the area where he found Maddie. "Have you seen a wallet? I think she said it was pink?"

"In this mess? Give me a few minutes." Tuttle continued snapping pictures. Joze couldn't stop shifting from foot to foot. He'd dive into the chaos and find it himself if it wasn't considered contaminating evidence. Anything to get back to Maddie pronto. But then what if this wasn't a real crime scene? What if it was a set up like before?

"Find anything important?" Sarcasm reigned. "Any real evidence to prove a crime actually happened?"

Officer Tuttle paused. "You don't believe the lady? You saw the bump on her head."

"Yeah, well..." It wouldn't be the first time she'd lied about something like this.

Tuttle turned back to the scene. "There were a few scuff marks where the grass got pulled out, but nothing else. It's hard to say under this trash."

No wallet appeared as the officers sifted through the trash.

Joze couldn't ignore the grinding rock building in his gut. Hmm. A missing wallet.

Officer Tuttle stood. Shaking his head, he glanced down the alley and back to Joze. "So, this is a robbery. Figures. There's been some heavier theft activity here lately. I'll put it in the report."

Joze resisted the urge to take off running. "Thanks."

He strode back toward the ambulance ensconced at the midway point of the carnival.

The slow spin of lights and carousel horses danced into view as he moved at a clip. He loosened his fisted hands. Since when did he get so caught up in emotions? God help him, he needed to let go of the past. And four years should be plenty of time to do so.

Two rides let out at the same time. People swamped him as they hurried to get to the next thrill. Someone knocked him forward. It took three steps to catch himself and keep from plunging headlong into the operator's little gearbox. "Hey."

He spun around as sharp pain shot across his shoulder blades and sent him to the ground.

"Stay away from her."

Joze jumped up and thrust around. The crowd was thick. People jostled each other, laughing and yelling. No one seemed to pay him any attention. His vision jumped from one person to the next, sweeping fast over the throng. No one stood out. Nothing looked anything but ordinary.

A man in a Patriot's hat hurried away. Joze charged in his direction only to see several others in baseball caps rushing in other directions.

His breath came out in jagged gasps.

Maddie wasn't lying this time.

He rounded the line to The Octopus Spin. Ahead, the interior of the ambulance lit the area around it. A second ambulance from the county rested beside his, and one of their EMTs had retrieved the girl with the smashed finger. She sat on the stretcher howling her head off, the arms of a woman wrapped around her. Before Joze reached his own vehicle, the ambulance driver closed the doors, climbed in, and pulled away.

Joze stopped at the doors of his unit and peered in. Maddie sat with her arms bolted tight to her sides. She did a good job of looking OK, but the pain was obvious in the squint of her eyes when she moved her head to talk to Jim.

He motioned for Jim to come out and then dipped his head when he drew near. "She's telling the truth about being attacked."

"I never doubted it." His co-worker pulled back. "Something happen to you? You're as pale as my grandmother's sheets."

Joze put his hand to his chest. "Yeah. Someone took a swing at me. Told me to leave her alone."

Jim's brows shot up toward his bald spot. "No way, man. Need an ambulance ride of your own?"

"I'm serious." Joze lowered his voice even more. "I'm going to stay with her, OK? I want to take her home."

"Sure. If she'll let you. But maybe she would if you told her what happened."

"No. I don't want to scare her."

Jim punched his shoulder. "Tuttle should be back to take her statement. Make sure you let him in on this, OK?"

Joze nodded. He studied Maddie a moment. She never turned in his direction. Instead she continued her tough-woman act. Why'd she always have to be so hard? Right now, no one cared if she let go of her façade. She was injured. What had she gotten herself into?

She swiped her hair out of her face and tucked it behind her ear.

He hung back a moment. Why had she blamed his best friend, Todd, for something he didn't do and ruin everything she and Joze had together? He steeled himself against the answer.

New day, new life. Forget what happened before. She could be a different person now too.

Her face fell when Jim turned away to organize the equipment in one of the cabinets. Scared? Tired? How could he have been so callous toward her when he came across her in the alley? She'd been attacked. A sudden desire to protect her took over the one to oust her from his life once again.

He grabbed the side bar to hoist himself into the vehicle and breathed in the familiar antiseptic and plastic tubing aroma that occupied his baby. Joze leaned down a hair. "No wallet. Sorry. Some thief attacked you."

Once again, a mask occupied her face when she turned to him. No need to worry her even more with the fact someone had gone after him too.

Should he tell her she had a piece of popcorn in her hair? "Officer Tuttle should be here in a few minutes. He's taking pictures of the crime scene right now."

She dropped her arms and slouched a tad. "I doubt he'll find anything with all that trash everywhere."

"If there's anything there, though, I hope he finds it." And he meant it.

She didn't look at him.

The ambulance seemed to shrink in size, bringing Maddie way too close to him in the confined space. He backed out and hopped down but didn't leave the edge of the path of light. The way her gaze shifted between the stretcher and the EMTs said she wanted to lie down. He shook his head. She wouldn't do it. Wouldn't show a moment of weakness.

Someone cleared their throat, and Joze jumped and spun around. Officer Tuttle. "Sir."

The officer stopped in front of the open bay. "Ms. Clare, are you ready to talk?"

Jim nodded and smiled assurance at her.

She scrutinized each one of the men. Her hand trailed back and landed on the popcorn in her hair. Joze held in a chuckle as she pulled it free and grimaced at it. He held out his hand. "I'll dispose of that for you."

She gave him a sideways glance, pursed her lips, and dropped it in his open palm.

Yeah, he should've told her it was there. The old Maddie would be furious that she didn't look perfect even after the event she'd been through.

She rubbed at her eyes.

5

Wouldn't Joze make sure she was embarrassed? What else was in her hair or on her clothes? She took a quick look at her shirt and swatted away a blade of grass. Green stains touched her jeans at the knees. *Please don't let there be pizza gummed on my back.*

The officer glanced around the bustling carnival, climbed inside the ambulance, pulled the doors shut, and sat beside her on the gurney.

Joze was definitely shut out. Good.

She repeated the account she'd told the EMTs, but this time more detail came to her.

He typed notes on his smart phone as she spoke. "Did you recognize the voice of your assailant?"

"No. He whispered. It's hard to say." She closed her eyes. The scene flashed into focus. Maddie pulled back and her shoulders tightened of their own accord. She couldn't take it in without sending her heart pounding in her chest like a crazy rock band drummer.

She opened her eyes.

He was watching her. "There's no need to rush. Take your time."

"Um." She squeezed the edge of the stretcher. "I don't think I've ever heard the voice before." *Stop shaking. Look him in the eye.*

Jim handed her a tissue. What for? Oh, her cheeks were wet.

She took it, swiped the tears away as fast as she could, and dropped the tissue beside her.

The officer sat in silence for a moment. "Even the smallest thing can help. Did you see his arm when he choked you?"

She bit her lip and nodded. Running her hand over the rough sheet that covered the gurney, Maddie tried once more to stop the fear from eating her inside out. "He was Caucasian."

When he finished questioning her, Officer Tuttle threw the doors open and stepped down. "I'll get back with you in a day or so, OK?"

"Good. Thanks." Her curt answer didn't make him turn back.

Joze stopped him and pulled him aside, as he had Jim. What was he up to? He talked a few minutes to the officer before letting him go. Officer Tuttle looked back at her and then typed furiously into his phone, alarm all over his pinched face.

He disappeared into the crowd after shaking hands with Joze.

Maddie scrunched her mouth. What was up?

Jim moved to the spot on the gurney the officer had occupied. Joze leaned in. "Listen, we'd all really appreciate it if you took our advice and let us run you to the emergency room."

Did she detect a note of empathy in his tone? What was going on? "I don't know."

Jim took her pulse. "I agree with Joze, ma'am."

Her first night home and she should spend it in the hospital? No way. The smell of the ambulance was enough to make her run. Couldn't the wonderful carnival odor take over the small space a bit more before she had to force herself up and out of the bay? "I thank you for what you've done so far, but I have to get home."

She started to stand.

Joze didn't move aside to let her down. "Can't you at least call someone to come get you?"

She felt around in her pockets but stopped. "I left my cell at home. Didn't think I'd need it."

"Well, you can borrow mine." Joze pulled his smart phone out of his pocket and offered it to her.

Maddie slapped it away. "No. I don't really have anyone to call. Mom's working late...I don't want to bother her."

"My ma would go nutso if I didn't call her right away in the same situation even though I'm a grown man."

He wouldn't understand. Mom was different—not the normal caring type of mother. She lifted a shoulder.

"My shift ends in ten minutes. Why don't I take you home?" His face remained blank, almost emotionless. "You shouldn't drive with a concussion. I could keep an eye on you if you're alone. For a while anyway."

Huh? First, he had nothing but disdain, and now he wanted to help? Maddie wrinkled her brows together and stared him down.

"So you can watch me, make sure I don't sleep?" Her tone boiled like acid.

"No. That's a common fallacy. You can sleep if you want." His calm voice ruined her steam.

It only took Jim a millisecond to jump in. "It'd be wise. He knows his stuff."

The third guy poked his head through the opening in the front. "Trust him. I'd let him take care of me."

Jim chuckled. "That's saying a lot, ma'am."

She wasn't going to get out of here if she didn't agree, was she? And her mom wasn't due home 'til late. It would be safer... But Joze? Of all the people to fall back into her life right now, why him? She squeezed the bridge of her nose. "Ten minutes?"

"Yep."

"Then I'm lying down for a bit." She steeled her face so he couldn't see how relieved she was to relax against the scratchy pillow that reeked of bleach.

As she shut her eyes, someone patted her arm. "Time to go."

What? "OK, but I just closed my eyes."

"It's been maybe fifteen, twenty minutes."

She attempted to jump up but stopped when the sharp pain in her head returned. "Wow."

Joze must've been the one to tap her awake. "I thought I'd give you a bit longer since you looked...comfortable."

Should she thank him? She kept her mouth shut. Wouldn't want to give him the impression she cared. She sat on the edge of the bed for a minute. Really, Joze? And let him in her mother's home?

Joze moved away. He was smart enough not to offer her a hand down.

Maddie took one slow step at a time until she knew she could trust her legs. She searched for the handle he'd grabbed earlier and took it with as tight a grip as she could. Everything seemed to be working again. Nausea gone. Dizziness at a bare minimum. Yet the jolly carnival music yelled at her as she left the cocoon of the ambulance. She dared not cover her ears. Wouldn't want Joze to think she needed more of his help rather than a ride home.

At least she wouldn't be alone after what

happened. Wasn't it a bonus to get over whatever made her want to tell him he couldn't? But he would be gone as soon as her mom walked through the door. She'd make sure.

With her head lowered, Maddie worked her way through the crowd and tried to call to mind the exact location of her car. Joze kept pace with her, always at her elbow but not quite touching her.

Maddie started to pass the carousel. One, two, three. Ah, there was her favorite horse, bobbing up and down with a small child aboard. She tried to keep a good march forward as she watched it swoop down and begin to ascend again, its teal mane ablaze in mystical off-shoots. But then she bumped into Joze. "Uh, sorry."

She crossed her arms and hoped she looked formidable, not like she was about to fall over. It gave her a chance to catch her balance and stabilize her vision.

Joze's gaze darted back and forth.

Maddie checked her surroundings too. What was she supposed to do, considering the only physical attribute of her attacker she could identify was his medium build? Lots of familiar faces floated in and out of her vision. But a ton of people who swarmed in from Hartford and surrounding areas filled the absolute recesses of the park.

Get moving. It would be safer behind the locked doors of home. Maddie didn't wait for Joze to catch up with her. With all the strength she could muster, she forced her legs into a trot toward the entrance.

No longer did the sweet air entice her. Its suffocating effects left her breathless in her flight. Someone could be following them right now. Right to her car.

Joze grabbed at her elbow but grazed her skin. "Hey, wait up."

He could keep up. His physique spoke of many hours in the gym. She didn't stop until the parking lot came into view. Which way? Had she parked to the left or right?

A man with a neon-yellow vest directed traffic. That's right, he'd been in the same general position when she'd arrived.

Maddie forced her body to move toward him. She riffled in her pockets for her key chain. It caught on the seam of the pocket and skittered to the stony ground.

Joze rushed to pick up the keys before she could brace against the sharp pain she would feel in her head if she bent down. A car blared its horn and stopped short. He stood and waved the car past.

"Sorry." She let him hold onto them. "My car's at the end of this row."

Several families flanked the row on their way to the park. She sidestepped a child not watching where he was headed. A woman reached out and pulled him close, eyeing Maddie.

When they reached her little hybrid car, Maddie sighed.

Joze unlocked the doors. "Same place you used to live?"

"Yeah." She ducked her head. Why had she brought him and another friend home for Thanksgiving all those years ago?

"Your aunt still live there too?"

Maddie blinked away the sudden moisture at the corner of her eyes. *Not still living there.*

6

Joze barreled down the highway in the tiny car with a dumb personalized license plate. Bugy Boo. Really? Who named a car something like that? Especially not Maddie with all her hard edges and perfectionist notions. He was kind of a small guy, but he had a hard time fitting in the cupped seat.

But this was for the good of another. He needed to stop being selfish and trying to find a way to keep her at arm's length the rest of the night.

And he'd blundered. Of course, her aunt wasn't still living with them. He'd been part of the recovery team for the small, downed commuter plane that crashed on its descent to the airport just over a week ago. Her aunt had been on the plane along with four other passengers. And Maddie had come home for the release of her aunt's personal affects and the funeral.

He cleared his throat and tried to turn to lighter conversation.

Storm clouds seemed to swirl on her face. "My aunt lived with us until recently."

He studied the highway signs and softened his tone. "Sorry. That was insensitive. I don't know why I asked. I'm aware of her passing."

She clinched her jaw. "Yep. Sure you are. I'm sure the whole town lines up every morning to get the gory details of the latest recovery item, don't they?"

Bitterness was her game? He glanced at her. "I'm sorry. I really am. She treated me like family when I visited, and I'd like to do the same for her, if I can." He shouldn't say too much. His superior hadn't given him the OK yet. "At her service…if it's OK."

Her curt nod and quick blinks shut him up. Why dig a deeper hole? To bury his already sinking chance at releasing the history between them?

Now wouldn't be a good time to tell her he knew all the details. And even some about her aunt's last moments.

He checked the side-view mirror before getting into the left lane. He passed a slow-moving eighteen-wheeler and began to return to the right lane when he took another peek in the mirror. Several vehicles had followed them for miles.

As he exited, a beige sedan took the exit with him. He did a double take. Now he was making things up. There wasn't anything unusual about it, so why make something out of nothing?

At the third stoplight, he turned right. His blood pressure built up in his veins and he squeezed the steering wheel. This was better than an action movie with all the adrenaline pumping in his body. Except he was responsible for a real life. Not something to take lightly.

"This road won't take you to my house."

Don't start questioning me now. "I thought you might need some pain meds." The drug store on the corner of a strip mall stayed open twenty-four hours every day. "Do you?"

"Right. I'm not sure what my mom has. I'll run in and get something."

He parked and jumped out. The beige car passed

the strip mall and disappeared. "I'm coming in too."

He peered around the side of the building and rubbed his hand across his chest. He needed to relax. There was nothing to get so excited about. He should be more surprised there weren't a few more cars following him back to the center of town.

She frowned. "If you must."

He swung around. What was that supposed to mean? Of course he had to. He couldn't leave her alone. That was the point of taking her home and waiting for her mother to get back from work. He bit his tongue. Thrusting the keys in his pocket, Joze hurried behind her. She moved at a fast clip. Must be feeling some better.

Maddie scanned the signs until she found *pain reliever* on aisle eleven.

A couple guys called out a hello on their way to the cash register. He answered back. It was nice to know most of the locals, but not always so great to know their medical problems. At least he had their respect.

With two bottles in her hand, Maddie headed to the front and plunked them down on the counter.

He drew close to her ear. "Want me to get those for you?"

She blew out a breath. "No. I got it."

Well, so much for being nice.

At the door, she slowed. "Sorry. Thanks for the thought."

"I'm not such a bad guy, you know. People change." But had she? When she didn't answer, he stopped. "Really."

She swung around and put a hand to her temple. "This whole thing has me on edge. I...apologize."

He stopped the urge to puff out his chest and declare a victory. "Let's get you home. That'll make things better." Unless the guy found them there now that he had her address.

She climbed in the passenger side of her car. He scanned the roads and then patted the roof of the car before squeezing inside.

They returned to Main Street, Joze constantly looked back through the mirror.

And there was the beige car. His heart pounded into overdrive again. Flooring the gas pedal to race up the hill, he slammed his hand against the steering wheel when the mini car refused to accelerate. It actually slowed with each passing yard. *Are you kidding me?*

Maddie smacked his arm. "Hey. Don't beat my baby." She looked around. "Wait, what's going on?"

He didn't want to scare her, but she'd never leave it alone. He squinted at a road sign as he passed. *Just get off the road. And quick.* "Don't go nuts on me, but I think a car might be following us."

Pulling the wheel hard, he took a quick right onto Plum Lane. Would it continue to follow? He'd have to call into dispatch if this didn't stop. "It passed us earlier but now it's behind us again."

"No, no, no." She bounced against the doorframe as the car revved on the turn. Her hands shook. "This can't be happening. I wondered…"

Again, he made a sharp turn, and she ducked down in her seat, her breath coming out so fast it hissed.

As bad as he wanted to read every subconscious cue on her face, he kept his gaze on the road and made a quick left. This was a new level of crazy. "Wondered what? Speak quick."

"My aunt—she wasn't acting right before she left for Chicago on a business trip."

He'd beat it out of her if it'd make her tell him faster. "Uh huh?" Keep going. Please. Now. "And…"

The wheels squealed as he slammed the brakes before hitting a rut in the road and then zooming back up to speed, his pulse racing as fast as the rising speedometer.

She stammered, "I don't know. She was troubled about something. She didn't say what."

He took another right when the lights of a car bounced from a dip in the road and shined in his eyes through the mirror. If this was the same guy, he was good. "Get down more. I don't know what's going on, but I want you safe."

She slumped further, grasping the door handle with one hand and her head with the other. It'd be bad to injure her even more with his sudden turns. But what choice did he have?

Another harried right turn followed by one more, and they were at a large intersection with a park and a road that encircled the whole place.

Had he lost the guy? He hadn't seen him make the last two turns. He should call in this situation, but would his buddies believe he wasn't pulling a joke on them? Now Joze regretted all his pranks on his PD friends.

He wheeled partway around the circle and parked between a cluster of cars—far enough away not to be seen by the driver but close enough to see if the car continued to follow. Only a couple street lamps lit the parking lot. Good—unless the car pulled in. His pulse thrummed at his neck as he scooted down a hair and held tight to his phone with his finger ready to push speed-dial to dispatch.

Maddie sat up an inch.

He put his hand on her arm. "Don't."

She slid back down. At least her car wasn't so unusual it couldn't blend in with the others. Should he find a parking garage to hide in?

There wouldn't be one open this late at night. Not in this small town.

Ten minutes passed before he loosened his tight hold on the steering wheel. It seemed like a hundred. He breathed hard, checking both entryways and every vehicle that went by. "I can take back roads to get to your house, but it's going to take a while."

She fidgeted. "Get me home safe, and I don't care." Maddie seemed to melt even more into her seat. "If he has my wallet with my address, why's he chasing us?"

"To scare you? I don't know." He wanted to believe it wasn't really the same guy. And practical sense said it had to be an unrelated driver just headed in the same direction, so maybe Joze had overreacted...

He eased back onto the road and went in the opposite direction, crisscrossing the highway and crawling down back roads.

Maddie kept quiet. He thanked God. Why add to the stress by fighting?

When they pulled into her drive, they both took a big breath and released it slowly.

She pointed to the back of the house. "Hurry. Head to the rear. There's a garage back there."

He did as she asked, and she pressed the button for the door to open. When the door closed behind them, Joze turned to her, the dark hiding her expression. "I need all the details on your aunt's situation."

Maddie patted the dashboard with motherly strokes. "Boy, you were rough on my baby."

Couldn't she enjoy his race car instincts for even a second, not to mention he may've saved her life? "How'd you afford this thing anyway?"

"I took a few years off to raise money for college and get this car. Not that it's any of your business."

Must've been after they'd parted ways, at the end of their sophomore year. Odd that it coincided with the supposed attack on her.

He pushed out of the driver seat to look out the high windows of the garage. No one. But the view was very limited. "Now start talking."

7

Maddie stopped the swing of her arm from slamming the door of the car. Joze's authoritative manner got under her skin. He was no hero to her. But hadn't he kept her safe on the ride home? It counted for something. The thought took the steam out of her next words. "Take it down a notch, Joze."

She rounded the car and reached for the garage's side door that led to the backyard of lush flowerbeds.

He yanked her close to his side and lifted himself up on his tiptoes to see again through the window.

"Stop," she said sharply.

"I thought I saw someone. Be quiet." His own voice lowered to an urgent whisper.

There was no way she was tall enough to take a look. She stiffened her body. "Let go of me. I won't go anywhere, you can be sure."

He never looked away but released her. "Got any weapons, shovels, hammer, anything like that in here?"

This was getting out of hand. Did he really need something deadly to defend them? She rubbed the goose pimples climbing up her arms. What had her aunt been involved in? And what did it have to do with her? "No. Auntie Lonna keeps those things in her gardening shed by her office." Her eyes stung. "I mean kept."

"Figures," he said under his breath. "Get your key out. I want to get you in the house as quick as possible."

He took one last look and then pressed against her as they rushed through the door and ran to the back of the house. Maddie forced her body not to react to his closeness. She thrust the key into the lock and twisted it open. They hurried in and slammed it. Joze pulled down the blind and put his head against it for a moment. "This is not how I thought I'd spend my night."

"Me either." Coming home shouldn't have to be a death defying act. And it never had been before. The strain of the day built up in her chest. *No tears.* Maddie repeated the mantra over and over until the threat of them dissipated. "What now? I don't want to scare my mom." Ha, would her mom even believe her? "But she has to know."

He moved into the spacious kitchen. New granite countertops accented the white cabinets. Bright blue paint kept the room from being too girly. "Call Mrs. Clare and ask when she'll be home. I want to be able to see her pull in."

"She told me earlier she'd be back by eleven." Running through the house, Maddie checked the front door to make sure it was locked. It hadn't been common practice in their household to lock doors when she lived at home. Had it changed? Nope. The door was unlocked. She threw the deadbolt into place also.

Maddie called out to Joze over her shoulder. "We need to make sure all the windows are secured.

They went room by room, checking and locking all possible entries.

This was a nightmare. How could she convince Mom that the house now had to be locked up like Fort Knox?

They stopped in the foyer. "Oh." Maddie scrunched her shoulders. "The basement has a rickety old door. And some windows. But I think I can get it locked if you push it hard for me."

Why did old houses always have to be so outdated when it came to basements?

As they moved down the steps, musty basement odor met Maddie's nostrils. She held the splintered railing and crouched low to see into the space below, almost bumping Joze as he stood in front of her. The low basement ceiling meant fewer stairs to descend. Wouldn't want him to stumble because he expected more. "There are only eleven steps. Be careful," she whispered.

"Thanks for the warning."

There wasn't a light switch to illuminate the area. They'd have to go to the center of the room and pull the cord.

She reached for the back of Joze's shirt in case she needed a shield, but she didn't touch him. He turned as if he knew. Man, her tough woman act was suffering tonight.

She shrugged. "What?"

A smile played on the corners of his lips as though he was trying to hold it in.

"Shut up." She scowled.

"I didn't say a thing."

Their steps weren't slow enough. Joze doubled over, falling onto something. "Umph."

Maddie had been hovering too close and tumbled beside him, managing to avoid contact. On her way down, she bumped the side of an old, burnt-orange couch.

Note to self—strangle Mom for changing the furniture around all the time.

His spicy cologne wrapped around her. A macho mix of goodness. She stopped the thought before it could ruminate.

Pulling herself up as fast as she could, Maddie tripped on Joze's leg.

"Ouch." He scrunched into a ball, grabbing his leg.

"Sorry. Give me a minute." She reached up and waved her arm around until the silky pull string fell into her palm. Light filled the room when she yanked.

Joze balanced on his knees, pushing himself upright. He strode to the back door, put his weight against it and locked it. "This door needs to be replaced."

It was a burglar's dream come true for sure. "I know. Mom hasn't stepped into the twenty-first century on the whole danger thing. It isn't like it was when she was young."

Maddie checked the windows.

Joze looked out the one side window closest to the front of the house. He shot his hand up, pointing at the light. "Quick, turn it out."

"What'd you see?" Her heart rate skyrocketed and she jumped for the string, cloaking them in darkness. She dared not move from the spot. No need to fall again.

"Someone's walking along the road."

What if it were only the neighbors? They were always outside with their dog. "But I thought you lost the guy with your super driving. Do you see a dog with them? Could be one of my neighbors."

"No."

Maddie ran her hands along a chair and took light steps until she passed it and a few boxes. The low light from a street lamp fell across Joze's face. She reached his side.

"They paused and looked this way a second ago. We should call the police."

He didn't have to tell her twice. "Come on. There's no phone down here."

Once their eyes adjusted, they moved a little better.

In the kitchen, Maddie grabbed the phone and dialed 9-1-1. How should she explain to the lady on the other end that they thought they'd been followed and now the perp was possibly walking around outside her home? She sputtered.

Joze took the phone from her. "Hey, Karen. It's Joze." He paused as the dispatcher spoke. "I'm with a friend." Maddie crossed her arms and stared him down. He put a hand up and shrugged. "We had some trouble at the carnival earlier, and then someone may've followed us home. I think he might be outside the house." Pause. He motioned for her. "House number…"

"Three-four-three-six," she spit the numbers out. Of course he would know the lady on the other end — and get to play hero again. Didn't he have that persona down?

When he hung up, Maddie pressed against the far side of the island. "What'd she say?"

"They're sending out a patrol officer."

"And we have to sit and wait? How long?"

"Don't know. I assume that, because of the carnival, it could take a bit for them to get out here.

Those events suck resources."

Maddie fought the urge to rampage. "What if the person breaks in while we're waiting?"

His hand went to the EMT emblem on his uniform. "You've got me."

She smirked.

He took in the room. "Seriously, stay close."

Great. To be close to him was one of the biggest self-betrayals she could think of.

He leaned back, resting against the counter. "Please tell me there's a gun in this house, or an axe—"

"Ha ha. So you can play 'axe murderer'?" She made air quotes with her fingers. "Of course there isn't."

He left her in the kitchen.

"Wait up. Where are you going?"

"To keep an eye out at the window. Come on."

Was she like a lost puppy following him like he commanded or what? It rankled. But what choice did she have?

Her hand trailed the chocolate-brown-stained wood paneling as they moved through the hall to the front of the house. Her mother hadn't opened the curtains that morning. At least the perp couldn't watch their movements.

Joze pulled the edge aside as she flipped the light on. "Please, leave it off."

She stood frozen in the doorway. "Are they still there?"

"No." He motioned for her to move to the other room. "Go across the way and check out those windows on the side of the house."

She planted her feet. "You want to boss me around?"

"Just go. I'm not trying to."

Maddie moved as stealthily as she could into the small library, guided by a small amount of light that moved down the hall and landed in the doorway. The windows of the Greek Revival home weren't quite floor-to-ceiling, but pretty close. She peeked through the thick plantation-style blinds. Black shadows covered half the expanse between her house and the neighbor's, too dark to make out a single form separate from the bushes and flowers. "I don't know, Joze," she spoke only loud enough for him to hear. "I can't tell. You should come see."

He was beside her so fast she jumped, and her hand went to her heart. "Whoa."

"Didn't mean to scare you." His shoulder grazed hers.

For the first time she studied his profile. Wow, he'd gotten even more handsome since she'd last seen him: his jaw a little broader, his cheekbones more defined.

He blinked and turned. "I don't see anyone, but it's hard to say."

Maddie closed her slack jaw and looked back out the window. "Uh huh."

Ten minutes later, lights flashed down the street and shot toward the house in a blue and white blaze.

She crumpled against the window frame. Safety. Here at last.

It took him a second to move away from her, an unreadable expression on his face. At the door, they waited for the officer to check the perimeters. Joze threw the door open when the policeman returned.

The officer's face split with a smile. "Joze, what're you doing here? I heard you were involved in this."

Joze ushered him in.

Maddie tilted her head to the side. Was there anyone he didn't know in the Hartford County law enforcement and emergency departments?

"Beaucamp, good to see you." He ran a hand through his dark hair.

The officer turned to her. "You are Madeline Clare?"

"Yes, sir." She tried to shake the flustered heat in her face. "I don't understand what's going on but," she had to swallow her pride, "thanks to Joze, I've been safe. He's right, someone has been following us."

He spread his feet and took an easy stance. "I checked the area. A few people walking dogs and such, but nothing suspicious." He eyeballed Joze and then her. "Either one of you get a good look at this person or persons following you?"

They glanced at each other and spoke at the same time, "No."

Joze put a hand to his waist. "I could tell the person on the street was definitely male. But I couldn't see any details from the window in the basement. And he didn't have a dog with him."

Officer Beaucamp nodded. "I heard about the report on the incident at the carnival tonight. Ms. Clare, have any other details come to mind since you spoke to Officer Tuttle?"

"No. I wish I could tell you more, but it happened too fast."

Joze reached out and squeezed her forearm. She gave him a weak smile, and for the first time, didn't want to move away. She gulped. Not good.

8

What next? Maddie reached for two glasses and filled them with ice and water to keep busy and not think about all the whys of tonight. She handed one to Joze and set hers on the granite counter, avoiding the crumbs from her mom's breakfast meal. The curtained windows of the kitchen kept the dark at bay. She tried to keep her eyes open, but between stress and a possible concussion, she was awake on borrowed time. "A patrol through the night will be plenty."

He squared his jaw. "But I should stay anyway."

What would Mom think of him staying? What did she think of it? The idea became more and more welcome after the events of the night and the possibilities to come. But she couldn't let him. Now, if he had a work partner she could lean on, things would really be looking up. Just as long as it wasn't him. Maddie hung her head. That wasn't nice at all, even if he couldn't hear her thoughts. "Mom should be home in less than an hour. I won't be alone. And you have your own life. Get back to it."

He glanced to the wall clock above the kitchen sink. "If I talk to Mrs. Clare and she agrees, can I stay?" He formed a perfect triangle on the countertop with his hands. He leaned in and out as he spoke.

Heat climbed up her face. Joze in the same house. Yesterday, she'd have said over her dead body. But still…bad guy out to hurt her versus Joze? She pictured the mental weights in each of her hands. "I'll make a deal with you. If I even suspect something bad is going down, I'll call you. Give me your cell number."

His mouth tightened, eyebrow raised in an evil glint. "Nice try to get my number, chick."

She'd have smacked him if he stood any closer. "Stop joking."

His hands went up. "Sorry. I guess you have a reason to be touchy tonight."

"Ya think?" She crossed her arms and narrowed her eyes.

He finished his water, slapped the glass down, and winced. "Didn't mean to do that." With a lighter touch, he pushed the cup toward her. "I'm staying—at least till Mrs. Clare gets here."

She dropped her arms and picked up her own glass. A patrol circling every hour or so was something, but a lot could happen in that time. "Deal." She drew out the word. "But then you go."

"Tell me you're going to have a security system installed tomorrow. I don't want my next call to be this address with your lifeless body on the floor—" He bit his lips. "That statement could be misconstrued."

She cleared her throat and took another gulp of water. The fluid cooled her throat. He had a way with words for sure. It didn't surprise her that he added double meanings to lots of things he said. It was no different than before. And the past could not repeat itself.

"So…" Joze looked around. "I want to know about your aunt. You didn't even mention anything about her to the authorities, did you?"

Stall. Oops. She'd forgotten to call Mom. She held

up a finger. "Let me find my cell phone." It wasn't really stall tactics—yes, it was. "I need to see how long my mom's going to be."

She rummaged through the miscellaneous drawer by the back door. Not there. Why'd he need to know anything? Once he left tonight, he wouldn't be back. And she'd make sure Mom had a decent security system. It would all be fine. She scurried to the hall and looked through the key basket on the mirrored coat rack and stand. There it was.

But was tonight a fluke? Would whoever had been following them realize she was the wrong person?

Maddie returned to the kitchen, speed-dialing Mom as she walked.

"Hello, Maddie." The usual distracted voice of her mom sounded no different tonight.

"Hey, when are you getting home?"

"I'm on my way. Hold on a minute." Rustling echoed through the phone. A pause. "Getting on the highway this late at night shouldn't be so hard. The traffic is bad tonight."

"Wait 'til you get to Anby. The carnival is probably closing down soon."

Joze moved closer to her, but Maddie shooed him away. "So...well...speaking of the carnival, I had an incident out there tonight."

"Meaning what?" Honking accompanied the question. Mom was a terror on the road.

"Someone grabbed me," Maddie rushed on, "and I kinda got knocked out." She squeezed her eyes closed. Mom would either be outraged or doubtful, and Maddie didn't prefer either outcome.

"How do you get yourself into these situations?"

"I didn't—"

Joze stole the phone from her. "Mrs. Clare, this is Joseph Evans."

Maddie could hear her mom's voice buzz through the air as if Joze had put the phone on speaker.

Maddie winced.

"It's true," Joze continued. "Maddie was attacked, and it wasn't her fault—"

Maddie grabbed for the phone. He twisted around and held her at bay with his left hand. "I'm keeping an eye on the situation until you get home...because we were followed when we left the park."

A sound reverberated out of the phone that Maddie assumed was her mother yelling.

Joze cut her off. "Ma'am. I'm only trying to help. Maddie shouldn't have been driving alone. I was only providing a medical service."

He raised his brows as he looked at Maddie

She pulled away and dropped her shoulders. Why hadn't she figured Mom would kick into overdrive and take him down a notch? Maddie held out her hand for the phone.

"Yes, ma'am. I understand. Here's Maddie." He handed it back.

Even at twenty-six, Maddie was still a teenager in her mom's eyes. Funny, since her mother had never been around to do the job when Maddie was young.

Now, if Maddie wanted to accept Joze's help, she would. And Mom had no say, now or ever. "Listen, I'll talk to you when you get here. Joze is staying and that's it."

He grinned and fist pumped the air.

Maddie made a face at him. "Bye, Mom."

She clicked the phone off and set it on the counter in a slow, deliberate motion, refusing to look at him.

"What did she say to you? Or do I want to know?"

"Let's just say she remembers the past, or at least a version of it."

Heat shot through Maddie's veins. Why wouldn't he see the truth? As much as she tried to will away the old pain and anger, it still surfaced. Slamming her hands on the counter, Maddie's voice went up a notch in volume. "How dare you—"

"Oh, come on. I don't want to deal with this right now." His hands flayed out in front of him.

As she stormed toward him with fists raised, Joze pulled her against his chest, holding her wrists tight in one hand. Too tight. His hand snaked around her waist.

"Ow. Let go," she growled.

"Fine have it your way. We're having it out, once and for all. Now." Everyone was yelling tonight.

Maddie tried to shove away, her gaze glued to his in a fierce scowl. What good would it do to bring up the past when Joze obviously hadn't changed his opinion? It only made the hurt jump back to life.

He had to leave. And now. "Just go. I don't want you here."

His breath went jagged. "No. What really happened? I want the truth, Maddie."

The heat of his body invaded her own. His muscles bulged like tight rocks against the flesh of her side at the strain of holding her thrashing movements.

She heaved a breath. For the third time tonight, she fought tears. Tears she refused to let fall. "You know the truth even if you don't want to believe me."

He pulled her even closer, their faces mere inches apart. His voice went dead cold. Quiet. "Todd would never do what you accused him of. I've known him almost my whole life."

"He wouldn't take advantage of a woman ever, Joze? Not ever?" She pressed her forearms against his chest to get some distance, but he only loosened a fraction. "Do you seriously believe that? You saw how he was around other girls." *Please believe me.*

His sweet breath touched her cheek. She blinked. How many times in the past had she longed to be in Joze's arms...before... But not now. Not when he wasn't budging an inch on the matter. With one sudden hard shove, she pushed him away. He took one step back but didn't tumble the way she'd planned.

She'd thought the hurt had been buried for good. How was it possible that her heart twisted and wrenched now? Once again Todd was the victim in his eyes, not her. She struggled to control the quiver in her voice. "You need to leave."

He reached for her again, but she moved fast enough to avoid him.

Joze crouched a hair. "I'm not going. We're going to talk about this."

She edged toward the hall.

He stood and ran a hand through his hair, taking one deep breath. "I'm sorry for letting this get out of control." Joze moved back a pace. "Please, let's go sit in the living room."

Maddie couldn't prevent a sniffle from escaping. "Why should I? It won't change anything."

He marched toward her and took her hand. His grasp was firm but not violent. "Please. I'm listening now."

Why must his warm palm on hers seem so right? She wanted to let go but couldn't. Maddie let him pull her to the couch, where she plunked onto it.

His swift gaze shifted back to the windows. He seemed to be listening to something. "Did you hear that? Let me make another sweep real quick."

Maddie froze against the cushions and strained to hear whatever had drawn his attention. No scraping or shuffling came from outside. Nothing.

While his back was turned as he looked out the window, Maddie wiped her face and tried to ease the tension in her body.

With one last look, he shook his head and moved away from the windows, sidestepping the coffee table to sit beside her on the edge of the leather sofa. "Go ahead."

She could still feel his arm around her waist, the whisper of breath on her cheek like little tingles. This whole thing was twisted. Shouldn't she be ready to punch him and take off, not pondering his touch?

He bent low and met her eyes with his. Maddie played with the ring on her right ring finger. His fingers lifted her chin. Why did this have to be so difficult? She took a shaky breath.

It was too painful to go back to that day. Too hard to think she'd allowed herself to be trapped. And by a friend, someone she trusted. How did she put it into words? She began in a whisper, "I wouldn't lie about this, Joze."

His mouth went into a hard line.

She faltered. "That day you'd dropped me off so you could work down at the coffee shop on campus, right?"

He nodded.

"Well, Todd wasn't in the mood to study like we planned. He wanted to go for a drive, and I was tired of trying to get him to pay attention to the discussion questions we were supposed to be answering."

He put his hand up, his knee bumping her as he did. "You were the one who wanted to go for a ride."

Why couldn't he see the truth? She squeezed her hands into fists and held her breath. "No. It. Was. Him. Period."

He gave a curt nod, but his eyes still held an ounce of unbelief. "And…"

"And so I gave in and went." She forced herself to keep talking, working against the growing pressure in her lungs. "I didn't think anything of the trail he drove to. All of us had been there before." She covered her mouth for a moment. Then she dropped her hand. Oh, how it hurt to remember. "And he started talking about how much he liked me. Still, at that point, I never suspected he would—I didn't even know he liked me as more than a friend." She squirmed and shivered, the old terror rising in her throat like the remnants of a bad burrito.

He put his hand up. "You're trying to say he liked you. No, no, you liked him. You betrayed me by trying to convince him to date you. You seduced him."

"Nooo…" She couldn't breathe or stop the prick of unshed tears. "That is not what happened." Maddie wanted to beat the truth into him with her fists. "No one believed me. Not even my own mother. You said you wanted to hear the truth. Well, here it is. Listen."

9

Joze wanted to strangle Maddie tonight. Just like he'd wanted to the last time he'd seen her. The air in the room suffocated him. A potpourri heater pumped out some syrupy-sweet aroma, and he wanted to gag. He pulled on the top button of the white shirt of his uniform as he sat beside her. Then he restrained his hands in his lap.

His best friend, Todd, had been by his side since he could remember. Todd would never try to steal Maddie from him, much less attack her. Joze couldn't wrap his head around her accusations, even with years between the most awful day of his life and now. He pushed down the urge to storm out and never talk to her again. But hadn't he promised her a fair hearing tonight? Hadn't he told God he would forgive her and move on? Her story hadn't changed. But...heat refilled his capillaries again. Todd was innocent. He knew it at his core. "Why would Todd do that to you? Why?"

She dropped her eyes and pulled back, their knees no longer making contact. The movement removed the heat between them and cooled the room to sub-zero. "I. Don't. Know." Tears leaked down her face in torrents, a sob escaping. "I don't get it either." She paused. "At least he didn't—"

He pressed a knuckle into his eye socket. Would she still be so torn up if she was lying? Her outpouring of tears dammed the anger welling in his chest. He needed to think, to step away from the situation and evaluate it again. "I—"

The front door handle jiggled. In a split second, he was on his feet and blocking Maddie. She shuffled behind him. "What's that?"

"The door. Please tell me you don't keep a spare key under a rock out there."

"Maybe."

Great. The bad guy could walk in anytime he wanted. Why hadn't he thought to ask her about a hidden key before? And there was no time to go into the virtues of never leaving keys where common criminals knew to look. "Stay behind me."

She shifted. "Don't boss me."

Did she want to die tonight? He didn't have time to argue with her about the benefits of listening to him for once. He sprinted to the hall and smacked into the door, turning to press his back against it.

She rushed to his side and pushed against it as well.

"You have your cell on you still?"

"No. It's in the kitchen."

Right. She'd set it down when he'd—no time to think about what he'd done.

The handle moved again.

A muffled female voice came from the other side. Joze met Maddie's gaze. He turned to look through the peephole and melted against the door. "It's your mom."

They jerked away and backstepped a few paces. Joze grabbed his chest. If he didn't stop jumping like a girl, his reputation would be at stake.

The front door squealed open. "I'm home. What's

going on?" Mrs. Clare stopped in mid-stride. She looked from Maddie to him and then dropped her keys into a glass bowl on a small table, creating tinkling as they settled.

He shifted from foot to foot.

Maddie wiped her face on her sleeve in one quick motion. "Mom."

Stay? Go? The awkwardness would fly through the roof if Mrs. Clare detected the tears on her daughter's face. And he was at the root of them. He flew to the window and took another hasty look. All clear. Better leave. He could set up a stakeout later. Wait a minute. Why do that? Maddie made it clear she could handle herself. Yet why couldn't he make himself walk out the door?

Maddie headed back to the living room.

He moved back to her side when he saw the lost little girl in her eyes. It tore at him to see her like that. A few droplets of tears rested on Maddie's shoulder. He smoothed them away before her mom could notice them. The rigidness of her body melted with the look. His hand lingered there a moment, the old attraction playing havoc on him.

Maddie's face contorted into a mask of blankness. She turned away.

Mrs. Clare dropped her briefcase at the doorway to the living room. "I don't have time for this right now. With the death of my sister, all the details left to take care of, I can't handle one more problem."

Maddie tensed. "I could leave. That'd be one less problem for you."

Her mother came over to her. "I'm sorry. I didn't mean it like that. Tell me again what happened. I'm just so exhausted."

They both sat, and Maddie began to recount the events.

Joze thrust his hand in his pockets and crossed the room. An alcohol wipe packet once forgotten lay at the bottom of one pocket. He rubbed it between his fingers. So this was what being a third wheel was like.

Maddie looked over at him. Hostility? Uncertainty? It hovered around her eyes.

He shuffled to the hall. If he didn't get some sleep, tomorrow would be a nightmare. Not that he'd be able to, with all the acid in his stomach. Better call Jim to drop him back at his car.

He studied the floor for a minute. Whether he believed her or not, she needed him right now. What if the attacker came back to do her more harm? "I'm going to head out. Let me know if there's anything I can do for you, Maddie."

She sat back. "I didn't get your number."

"Right." He ticked it off.

Mrs. Clare crossed her arms. "I'm sure we won't need it."

Didn't Maddie say even her mother didn't believe her about Todd's attack? Mrs. Clare sure acted like she believed it.

Maddie got up. "I'll walk you to the door."

Joze looked from Maddie to her mother and back to Maddie again. "Okay, bye."

Mrs. Clare returned his wave with a sour look.

Once outside the door, Joze stood toe to toe with Maddie. "I want to finish that conversation. Call me. And call me if you need anything else. I don't actually live that far away. Can I come by tomorrow?"

Her arms and legs were crossed tight, her lips pinched together. "I don't know." She looked around.

"How are you getting home?"

"Don't worry about it. I'll call Jim to pick me up."
He suddenly remembered her aunt. "And we need to
figure out how your aunt might play into this mess."

"No. I do." But her words weren't steely hard like
before.

Their closeness was like the scene from a first date
good-bye. Minus the love and euphoria...and mutual
attraction. He grimaced. Okay, it wasn't anything like a
first date. Except he was close enough to kiss her. And
he couldn't deny the attraction on his end no matter
how hard he wanted to make it go away.

And who in the world was thinking of kissing? He
placed his hand on the back of his neck as he took a
backward step.

Liar.

10

The singed ground left its black scent in the air and its black marks in the treads of Joze's work boots. Why wouldn't the morning sky light up with colors to make his job a little easier?

O' six forty five. He worked in the glow of halogen spotlights on the recovery grid of a downed small, passenger plane. Shouldn't the sun have already started working its way up in the sky? Maybe rain was on the way.

He pushed away a snarl. Too little sleep. Worry chewed on his insides all night long, even in his dreams, and kept his mind on Maddie. Before he'd gone to bed, he'd hooked up his police scanner and turned the volume on high to listen for any problem at Maddie's place. Then he'd forgotten to turn on his alarm, so he had to do seventy-five miles an hour down the highway, God forgive him, to get to the site in time.

As he worked in the constricting square on the hillside, Joze couldn't come up with a decent way to keep an eye on Maddie. Thank the Lord she hadn't needed to call the police during the night. Hopefully, that meant she was safe—and sleeping—at the moment. And he circled back to why he should care either way.

Something deflected light from his flashlight. Joze

bent down and brushed at it with nimble strokes. A chunk of metal began to show as the dirt cleared away. He stuck a red flag next to it, marked it on the paper grid he carried on a clipboard, and swung his light around to see if anything else lay in the same general vicinity.

Once again, a glimmer of light caught on a small object. He brushed the dirt away. A locket, half-burned, came into view. Another red flag. Another bit of sorrow for the family members pressed back into place.

He finished the grid and called the head officer to send the crime scene photographer over to document the items.

It'd been days since he'd turned up body parts. And he couldn't be thankful enough for the reprieve. At last count, six of the seven passengers and crew were accounted for. Over a week of work from a crew of fifty volunteers they were getting close to releasing to family members what was left of the passengers and their belongings. That meant Maddie and her family would be on the receiving end this week. He shook his head and glanced up at the tiny ray of morning sunlight that seemed to land on him alone.

This was sacred work.

One of the commanding officers called him away from the second grid he'd stepped into. He moved at a fast clip to cover the distance to the nearby warehouse that had been commissioned as a temporary morgue and debris storage area. At the entrance, he stopped at a table where his commanding officer sat typing on a laptop. "Sir?"

"I heard your request for a Lonna Selby to be put in your care. Is this a family member?" The commander frowned.

"No sir. A friend's family member." Joze took a wide stance, hands and clipboard behind his back. That wasn't exactly the truth. But how could he explain his relationship to the deceased otherwise?

"I've contacted her closest family member and made arrangements for the body." He said it like she was a piece of meat. A hazard of dealing with death too often. "But we also found some belongings in a fire-resistant case." He stepped back to a table and eyed a pile of paperwork. "Would you like to deliver her personal belongings today?"

Would he? This would give him an excuse to check on Maddie. Not that he wanted to diminish the importance of his true mission to give her Lonna Selby's things.

He signed the documents the officer handed him and waited as the officer gave the location listing to another recovery worker. Minutes ticked by. Workers came and went. Deposited plane pieces and other items here and there. All so scientific.

At last, a woman carried out a cardboard box the size of a medium bin. "Here." She checked the number on the box to the paper in her hand. "Thank you for your service."

"And you yours." He gave her the same sad smile she shared with him and then turned and left.

In the time he'd been in the warehouse, the sun rose in brilliant purples and pinks as if it waited just long enough for him to step back outside. Then the colors began to fade and full sun took their place. He hesitated in the doorway to take it in. Today should be his day off, but the possibilities were already filling it up.

It hadn't occurred to him in the beginning of the plane recovery that Maddie would be a factor in the return of her aunt's belongings. His only thought was to give Mrs. Lonna her due respect since she'd welcomed him and treated him like one of her own kids when he'd come to visit for Thanksgiving one year when he and Maddie were dating. Now there was a whole other dimension to the situation.

Was it too early to arrive at Maddie's doorstep? He calculated the drive time. He'd be there by 8:00 AM. if he didn't hit too much traffic. Leaving the Hartford area wasn't as bad as the west-bound side of the highway would be.

He set the box down in his truck with careful reverence.

Please let Maddie answer the door...and not Mrs. Clare.

11

Ominous gray clouds threatened to overwhelm the sun. Maddie sat in her old bedroom staring out the window. Rain. What'd they say about April showers? But please not today, even if the flowers needed it. And her aunt's beloved garden certainly could use the water. The daffodils and pansies had sprung up in colorful clumps. Who'd tend them now? Mom was too busy with her real estate business. Maybe she'd hire a gardener.

Maddie wiped her face. Poor Aunt Lonna. She'd been her real mother figure. All the years of hanging out on her bed and reading together with her cousins or dancing to old records were gone. And right when Aunt Lonna was about to have a new chance at life.

Maddie dropped the curtain and slumped onto the low vanity seat given to her by her grandmother. She should be doing homework or finishing the ten-page research paper due for her Psych class in two weeks. Graduation was only a month away. Then real life could begin. She wouldn't be the "forever" student anymore. Even the new job at the environmental and health safety office started in July.

Maddie stared into the four-foot mirror of the 1940's vanity with its faux mahogany finish. Whew, she needed some makeup to hide the exhaustion on her face. Eyes puffy and hair limp. But little sleep, which was interrupted by bad dreams, would do that to anyone. At least she'd had a productive morning. Mom had already taken her to the DMV to replace her license. Check. Two things done to get back to normal. Last night she'd called her bank to have her debit card locked and a theft alert added to the account. Now, she and her mother needed to finish the discussion about a new security system.

She rushed through applying some concealer and then headed downstairs. "Mom, please tell me you're still here."

Mom answered from down the hall in the master suite. "I'm in my room. I only have a few minutes, so hurry."

Maddie sprinted down the hall into her mother's powdery perfume-filled room. "Hey. We need to finish that conversation." She twisted her hair up into a bun and tied it with a hair band. "I can give you a list of all the reasons we should have a security system, or I could e-mail the one I compiled last night."

Mom waved the comment away. "I get it. Potential intruder returns. Yada, yada. Send me the security companies' numbers in the area when you get a chance."

All business, as usual. How did Mom hold it all in? Didn't she need at least one day to grieve over her sister and to face this new threat? "Fine. Look," Maddie played with a loose strand of her own hair, "the cousins are going to start arriving tomorrow. I don't want them to know about this whole mess."

"I get it." She picked up her curling iron and twisted a lock of hair around it. "If the system can be installed before they get here, nothing needs to be said." She pulled the rod away and let the curl bounce. "I could ask Rod to stick around."

Not the old ex-boyfriend that still showed up from time to time. "I don't think that's necessary."

Her mother curled another fake blond strand. Maddie watched her through the mirror. Why couldn't she be the mother she should've been?

Mom dropped the curling iron, turned it off, and sprayed a liberal amount of hairspray around her head. "Gotta go. I might be late." Nothing unusual about that. "Think you'll be OK here alone? What do you think of this new eye shadow? Too brown?"

Maddie missed Aunt Lonna even more. "It's fine." But she couldn't take another hour of waiting at the window to see if the perp showed. Mom didn't really care. "I'll be fine."

Mom dropped a peck on her cheek at the door. "Like I said, send me the list. I'll get right on it."

Maddie pushed past her and took a hard look around the street and yard. "OK. It's safe. Go."

Her mother sighed and shook her head. "Bye."

As she rested against the back of the door, Maddie touched the wood where Joze had been only hours before. Was he on the brink of believing her?

When they'd been on the porch as he was leaving, she was sure he'd considered kissing her...at exactly the wrong time. But then he pulled back fast. She touched her lips. That wouldn't have been OK. She didn't even know where she stood with him. And she didn't need him again.

Last night, Maddie couldn't start searching through Aunt Lonna's room with Mom around. She couldn't even tell her mom that she suspected the attack was related to her aunt and not anything she'd done. Her mother wouldn't get it or believe her. But Maddie'd picked up on the fear and trepidation she'd heard in her aunt's voice when she'd called to check on her only hours before the plane crash. Aunt Lonna wouldn't tell Maddie what was wrong, though.

Why hadn't she insisted on knowing what it was? Yet another failure on her part. But she wouldn't fail her aunt now.

Triple-checking the front and back door, Maddie hustled to Aunt Lonna's bedroom, cell phone in hand. She'd call the police if the slightest thing seemed off.

She stepped into the lavender-scented room. One of her aunt's homemade soaps created the aroma. She breathed it in and moved to the highboy dresser. A few pieces of jewelry and an antique silver brush, mirror, and comb set sat on a doily where they always rested.

Maddie looked under the bed, in the closet, and the nightstand. Nothing stood out. The desk was littered with papers and photo copies and an old year book. That's right, she'd been in the middle of helping to organize her thirty-year class reunion. Maddie flipped through the year book. Big hair and high-waisted jeans. Style that screamed the eighties. She set it back down.

In the top desk drawer, she pulled out a file and flipped it open. Papers regarding Aunt Lonna's newly acquired natural soap business were smattered with figures. She'd have to go out to the office in the backyard to find more info on exactly what her aunt's trip involved. The trip that ended in her death in a plane crash.

Maddie crumpled to the floor and hugged her waist tight as grief took over. So senseless. A dumb plane crash from a malfunctioning flap on the wing.

This wasn't the first time she'd delved into the agony of loss. There was another time she'd had to live with it. And that pain still showed its ugly head at the worst possible moments. Still deep and penetrating like a knife to the heart—the death of her father.

Today was not the day to bury her head under her pillow over something she couldn't change. She put back the folder.

Get up. Take some meds for the growing headache. Get out of the house. A nice public restaurant was the safest place to be. Maddie rummaged in the utility closet for a box of tissues. No way could she get through the day without it by her side. Where was the best place she could boohoo without being noticed?

She reached for the kitchen door handle. It turned in her palm.

Falling backward, she lost her balance and fell. The tissue box shot across the floor. Who was trying to open the door? Mom never made a return trip, even for important items. Not this quick anyway.

"I told you not to talk. I won't warn you again." A deep tenor voice echoed. The dark form on the other side of the door moved away.

She scurried on hands and knees to the other side of the kitchen island. The tile floor tore at her knees.

Get a knife. She shot up and winced at the pain in her knees. She rummaged through each of the drawers in a frenzy. Why'd Mom have to reorganize these too? Was it part of her coping mechanism?

The corner drawer flew open and threatened to spill all over the floor. Maddie stopped it in time.

The handle to the front door shook.

Finally, she gripped the biggest knife she could

find.

She pressed her back to the wall of the hall. Good thing the glass panes in the door sidelights were frosted. No one could see in. That also meant she couldn't see out unless she got on her tiptoes to look through the peephole.

Maddie eased forward. Where was a gun when she needed one? That would do the trick.

Somewhere to the left side of the house, a glass pane of a window rattled as if it might shatter. Boy, he moved fast.

Would she have a better chance if she made a run for the front door and raced to the neighbor's house? She figured the distance from the window to the front door. It might work, but it would be a huge risk.

Better not try.

She fumbled in her pocket for her cell phone, speed-dialed 9-1-1, and waited.

When the dispatcher answered, Maddie explained her situation and then kept the phone to her ear as she followed instructions to get to a safe hiding place. What about the basement? The door meant she could escape if need be. But the intruder could come in that way, too.

Maddie was torn. The knife handle in her hand began to chafe from her white-knuckled grip. Her legs threatened to give out under her. She slid down onto her haunches, braced against the wall.

To the basement. Hide in the small closet under the stairs. No, that would be too obvious if he managed to get in the house. The hope chest down there had been empty for years. *Please let it still be empty.*

Maddie stuffed the still-active phone into her pocket and dashed to the basement door, fairly slipped down all the steps, and ran to the chest. She threw the lid up with one hand. Blankets. Great. Feeling as though her heart were exploding, she yanked most of them out and tossed them on the old easy chair nearby. Then she climbed in.

The lid clunked down. She winced and waited. Scrunching under the remaining blankets, Maddie tried to slow her ragged breathing. She pulled the phone back out. "OK, I'm hiding."

The dispatcher tried to calm her. "Police should be there in three minutes."

Maddie begged her breathing to slow down.

The dispatcher told her she was checking something on her screen. "OK, a patrol officer is on your street."

She thanked the lady and hung up.

The doorbell resonated through the house, matching the beating of her heart. Maddie pushed a strand of hair out of her mouth and clambered out of the chest. She didn't loosen her grip on the knife. Taking the steps two at a time, she hurried to the door. Up on her toes, she stared through the tiny hole. Joze? What was he doing here? Then Officer Tuttle appeared behind him.

She checked around the foyer and decided to thrust the knife under the coats. He didn't need to know how dumb she was being. And for a second time in less than twelve hours. She shook her head.

Maddie rubbed the sweat off her palms onto her pants leg and opened the door. "What're you doing here?" Her gaze landed on the mid-sized box in his hands and her stomach dropped like a rock. The word *Official* was emblazoned on the lid, along with her aunt's name. Everything slowed around her. The buzzing of a neighbor's lawnmower seemed to die away. The patrol car lights paused in their flashing. Why'd Joze have it? It wasn't big enough to hold a full suitcase.

The officer talked into the radio mic at his shoulder then spoke to her. "Ma'am, are you OK?"

She couldn't look Joze in the eye. "Yes. He...he spoke through the door and said I shouldn't have talked." Another skitter of breaths shook out of her. "He went around the side of the house."

Tuttle nodded and took off in that direction.

Joze pulled her away from the door, the box balanced between his hip and left hand. His fingers went to her wrist. Was he checking her pulse? His gaze roved over her before he stared into her eyes then ran light fingers over the back of her head and neck almost as if on autopilot. "I guess it's confirmation he was here last night and saw us together."

She pulled back a fraction and put her hands to her temples. "Yeah. He was checking all the doors and windows."

Guiding her to the living room, he placed his hand at the small of her back as they walked. Oddly comforting coming from him. "I should've been here."

How could he have known the guy would return in broad daylight?

Her gaze went to the windows and then the box again. It was all too much. "My aunt's? I...I don't understand why you have it."

He paced back and forth, clutching the box. "I can't *believe* I missed the guy again. Did he say anything else? I can't believe this."

A shiver ran through her. She told him the rest of what the assailant said.

At that Joze stopped. "That's a threat. Something more has to be done." Joze went to the window and took a look.

"The trees are so close he could hide in seconds." Maddie pressed her hands against her sides to get them to stop shaking.

The officer returned and listened to her stilted tale. "Well, he's gone. I don't see any evidence to show he'd been back there, though. I'll file a report. Phone if you need us."

He hurried away to another call from dispatch.

File a report? What if...

She repressed a second shudder and shook her head. The bad guy was gone. For now.

Joze stood stalk-still, watching her.

Her gaze returned to the box. Maddie didn't know what to focus on. But the box would keep her from thinking about the stalker. And right now, she wanted to do anything but think about him. She looked at Joze, brows knit together. "Why do you have something with my aunt's name on it?"

He winced and stopped shifting back and forth. "I work for the recovery team near the airport where the crash occurred. I...wanted to do the honors of bringing this to you. It probably should've come up last night, but with all that was going on," he waved a hand, "I didn't think it was an appropriate time."

Wow, what could she say? It was hard to remain mad at him when he'd been so thoughtful. She reached for the box. "Can I have it?"

He handed it over, and she took it with care. The slight odor of burned paper came through the cracks. This was unreal.

If he wasn't standing there, she'd let the tears rip

again. Why was this happening to her?

He moved to sit in one of the easy chairs. "Didn't your mother let you know they were releasing Lonna Selby and her belongings today?"

"No," she faltered and fought the sting of tears. "I knew it was going to be sometime this week, though." She held in a curse against Mom. Didn't she know how this would affect Maddie? Didn't she care?

"Any problems last night?"

"Nothing." She stared at the box. Wasn't today enough?

The house phone rang. Maddie carried the box into the kitchen and set it down then took the phone off the base unit, Joze on her heels. "Hello?"

"Masterson Locks and Keys. We were called about an install today for a security system."

"Yes. That's right." Mom didn't even wait for her to send the info she'd asked for. At least she was taking the situation somewhat seriously. And now there was proof how much they needed the system.

The security guy gave her general information. She tried to push away the dream quality of the moment. The haziness slowed her brain. "Thanks. See you around two."

She hung up. Too many things bore down on her. Her head spun. "I need to sit down."

Joze followed her to the living room. She worked to look normal. Sucking in a few breaths, Maddie rested against the back of the couch. In spite of his effort to look casual in jeans and a polo shirt, Joze had an air of prestige. That was just like him to show her up with his cool attire while she looked dumpy in a big sweater. She glanced away. It wasn't a fair judgment. He didn't deserve meanness. Not after bringing her aunt's precious things to her, and possibly being the reason the stalker ran off.

He studied her from across the coffee table.

She broke eye contact after a second.

"Want me to get the box?" he asked.

"Sure." *Wake up, girl.* She shook out her hands.

He returned and set it between them. "I'd leave and give you some privacy, but until the security guys come, I'm staying."

She didn't have the strength to argue. Opening the box, Maddie peered inside. A scorched bag remained closed. She pulled it out. Aunt Lonna's carry-on with the nametag somewhat singed but intact. She unzipped it with care, avoiding the black burn marks on the edges. The back began to disintegrate onto the coffee table.

Joze knelt by her. "Want me to hold it while you pull the stuff out?"

She nodded, biting her lips. Her insides turned to mush. These were the last things Aunt Lonna had touched. She stroked each item as she pulled them out. The papers against the back were unreadable, black through and through. But other things were only burned a little. A sweater managed to survive mostly intact. She brought it to her nose. Aunt Lonna's smell was covered by a singed plastic odor. She set it down.

The last item, a small book, was missing the top corner. She flipped through it. Not a book, a journal. Her chest tightened. Aunt Lonna still wrote in a journal? Hadn't she given it up years ago? Maddie held the book to her heart. Joze scrutinized her. "What's that?"

"Aunt Lonna's journal."

12

Joze stared Maddie down. He wanted to fly over the coffee table and rip the book from her hands for a quick look but stayed in his seat out of respect. "There could be information in it to explain this crazy stalker situation."

He drummed his fingers on the table and squinted at the cover, his body buzzing. This would be the perfect time for X-ray vision.

"I wonder." Maddie opened the cover again. Then she closed it and put it back in the box.

"So you don't want to find out—like right now?" Joze inspected the box that wreaked of fire and aviation fuel.

She also bent to get a better look inside. Why was she holding back? "We need a name. And we need it now. Come on, let's read it."

She pulled back. "I want some privacy, if you don't mind, before I read my aunt's intimate thoughts."

Oh. "But keeping you safe is more important." Didn't she get it? "Can I at least take a quick look? I promise to skip anything…you know."

Maddie's words were clipped. "My aunt wasn't like that."

He held his hands up. "I didn't mean to suggest anything. But—"

"No, Joseph. I'll read it." There it was again. The formal use of his name. Which he hated.

He grabbed his head and groaned. "Whatever. It's not like a stalker isn't out there somewhere. Close."

She frowned. "You're right. What am I thinking? Things are getting serious."

Yeah, enough that she'd be hard put to get rid of him until things were figured out. Good thing he'd brought his gun this time.

She stood. "You know, I haven't gone to my aunt's office in the back. What if he got in there?"

He didn't wait for her to finish. "Come on. Let's see if anything was disturbed."

She headed to the kitchen and took a key from a drawer. "Should we take a knife with us?"

He put his hand to his back pocket. "I have something better."

She let her head fall back. "I'm going to have to get one of those for myself."

They moved to the backyard. A white building matching the columned front of the house took up the right corner of the property. There were a lot of amenities to this place. He guided her in front of him as he scoped the yard from side to side.

She tried the door handle. "Whew. It's still locked. That's a good sign."

He put his back to the wall by the entrance and waited for her to go in. At her elbow, he made sure he remained close.

Cabinets and shelving lined the room on every side. A staircase at the far end headed to an upper level. White walls. Beach getaway feel. A huge table took up the center of the room. "What'd your aunt do for a living?"

Maddie dipped down to look under it. "She just partnered with another company to expand her homemade, natural soap business. That's why she was...on the plane." She stood up and wiped at her eyes. "She'd met with them in Chicago."

"Anything going wrong with the merger?"

"Not that I heard, but I was at college. I'm sure there's plenty she didn't tell me."

He circled the table. "You said you'd talked to her right before she died. She didn't mention any issues?"

"No. She seemed excited about the business. Said everything was going better than she hoped. It was later in the conversation she sounded upset."

Don't take a break now. "And?"

She checked a closet in the corner. "Something about the reunion she'd been helping to set up."

A new factor. If it wasn't the business, did it have to do with the reunion? "You mean a class reunion or what?"

"Yeah, her thirtieth."

He went up a couple steps. What if the guy was still there? He tried to peek over the ceiling beams to the floor above. Nothing. Another wide-open room with the exception to a door in the corner. Papers littered the floor. A cabinet lay on its side. "Any relationships or issues with them?"

"I don't know. I bet it's in the journal."

Another reason to hurry up and get the thing read. Maybe Maddie didn't know her aunt as well as she thought.

They went upstairs. "I imagine your aunt wouldn't leave it like this?"

She grunted as she thrust her hands to her sides. "Oh, no."

Maddie bolted through the room. "Why would he lock the door when he left?"

"To throw us off." Joze stood at the window that started at floor level and stopped at knee height. A spatter of rain hit the window. "See, we didn't even get the police to check in here." He went to the large office desk. All the drawers were open. "I think we shouldn't touch anything. Take pictures and I'll call the officer back."

Maddie moved away from the turned over cabinet. "True."

He dialed Tuttle. "Hey, man. This is Joze Evans. We were checking things out after you left and found the office in the backyard had been broken into. You want to come back?"

They waited in silence for the officer to return. Joze eyed Maddie across the table in the downstairs room.

Officer Tuttle pulled up to the garage across the yard. Maddie and Joze watched him run through the rain to the tiny porch.

Another officer pulled his patrol car behind Tuttle's and followed him in.

Maddie sighed. For a second, he wished he could hold her up, bolster her through this, but he kept his distance. She gestured around the room. "When we first came in, everything seemed to be in its place down here. But upstairs, the place is a wreck."

The officers advised them to stay downstairs.

Joze moved to Maddie's side. "You doing OK?"

She put the tough act mask on. A warning not to get too close. "Yeah. I deal with this every day. What's to be worried about?"

Was she like this when he was in college with her?

Not that he could remember. Sure, she had a little edge to her but nothing like this. Hmm. "Ha-ha."

Tuttle came back down. "If you don't mind, you can go back to the house. We'll deal with this then come see you before we go. By any chance, have you noticed anything missing?"

She puffed out a breath. "My mom might be able to tell you, but I've been away at college. I wouldn't really know."

Tuttle nodded.

They returned to the house, running through the rain to get to it. Joze held the door open for her to go in front of him. Would Mrs. Clare be any help? It didn't seem like she kept up with much other than her business.

Maddie dropped onto the couch. "This nightmare's never going to end."

He reached for the journal and pulled it out of the box. Dare he sit beside her, or was it a safer bet to take one of the lounge chairs? At least by her side he could peek at the book as she read if she refused to give him access to it.

Maddie pulled it out of his hands. "Please. Respect."

Let it go. "Start at the back."

She dropped the book against her chest. "You act like you have some vested interest in this. You don't."

Oh, he did. Should he tell her? "You don't—"

She rested her head on her palm, elbow propped on the arm of the couch and watched him.

What should he say? He bit off another reply. How should he go about this? He rubbed the stubble on his jaw. "I didn't want to scare you even more after what you've been through…but the guy went after me at the carnival, too. When I went to find your cotton candy."

She sat straight up. "No way."

"Yeah." He scratched an itch on his cheek. "So now you know why I have to help you. It's me, too." Did that sound selfish? "I mean I'm a part of this mess."

Her gaze bounced between the journal and him. "I'm sorry." Hands went to her face. "I didn't know. Never even guessed. This makes me so angry." Then she studied him. "Is that what you were telling the officer last night back at the ambulance?"

"Yep."

"Wow. If this guy's willing to go after both of us, this has to be about something big."

True. "So are you going to let me help now? Without shutting me out?"

She finally sat back. "I don't have a choice. I want to know what's going on."

There was an element he couldn't believe he'd left out. God. Their safety, the whole thing needed to be bathed in prayer. What did he remember about her faith? He sat forward, forearms on his knees. She hadn't been remotely religious back then. It hadn't bothered him in college, but now? Maybe that would explain the change in her. She didn't have any faith to turn to when it was scary in this world.

Joze played with the idea of asking her. It'd put her through the roof for sure if the answer was still no. But...God deserved a place in this mess. "Look, we should pray about this whole thing."

She bounced away from him. "Don't get all religious on me. Since when did you believe in any of that stuff?"

"It's a long story." One he didn't want to repeat. It'd show her how far he had fallen before Jesus picked him up. "But we need Him right now."

She snorted and opened the journal, pretending to read it. But her eyes jumped around. She couldn't fool him. He lowered the top of the book. "OK, fine. You want to be in rebellion, have it your way."

She sputtered. "You want to see the journal, leave Him out of it."

So she blamed God? For what? Todd? Something else? "I'm giving this situation to God, one way or the other."

13

The drizzle outside the window matched Maddie's mood. She rested her forehead against the cold glass of the sidelight. Joze wasn't telling her what to do again. And he certainly wasn't bringing God into things, either.

But should she feel bad about throwing him out? This day had spiraled so far left field.

An inkling of regret tried to wheedle its way to her heart. No. He'd pushed her last button. She wasn't on speaking terms with God. And never would be.

And the stalker-slash-attacker could be waiting for the very moment the cops and Joze left her in the dust for all she cared before she'd accept His help again.

How ridiculous was she? And there were two hours before the security company was due to install the system.

The phone rang. She flinched. In the living room, she lifted the phone off the arm of the couch. "Hello?"

"Hey, Mad, it's Jocelyn." Her cousin's clear voice held tears in it. "I have a test to take today. Then I'll be heading to the train station. Aunt Sassie called to tell me the funeral is Sunday."

The old nickname Aunt Lonna had given Mom rang true on many levels. And none of the cousins had reverted back to her real name as they became adults.

It was so good to hear her cousin's voice. Really,

she was more of a sister. "Can't wait to see you. It's been too long."

"I know. With all of us scattered around the east coast it's hard to make it home at the same time." She choked a bit. "Can you pick me up? I get in around 10:00 AM tomorrow morning."

"Sure. I'll be there. It's the station in Hartford, right?"

"Yep. Couldn't get a direct route to town. When are the others due in?"

"By tomorrow night. Devin's taking a plane. No matter what we say."

"Whatever." Papers shuffled on the other end.

Maddie didn't want to hang up the lifeline. "Couldn't you take that test when you go back? I wouldn't want you to fail...with everything that's happened."

"I just want to get it over. Then I won't stress so much while I'm home." She cleared her throat. "That'll be enough to deal with. Hey, did you hear Aster's thinking of taking over Mom's new business?"

Maddie moved to the dining room and plunked into a chair. "No."

"Well, she graduates a week after you, and she's planning on going straight home to start figuring out the business."

"I'm kinda glad to hear it." Aster's degree would be in business. All Aunt Lonna had worked for wouldn't be a total loss then.

"I better go. Class starts in fifteen minutes."

"OK." She played with a string on her sweater. "Love you, bye."

She stared at the phone for a full minute.

She better leave the stress of the trapped house

and go to town.

"Hey."

Maddie jumped sky high, heart in her throat. "Mom. Don't scare me like that."

"Sorry." She drew the words out. "I forgot something, and a client insisted on seeing it." She headed to the kitchen and reached into the fridge to take out a bottle of water. "The security guys aren't here yet?"

Maddie followed her and put her full weight against the island. "They're scheduled to be here around two. I was just headed out."

"Oh, you're going to be back, right? I can't deal with them today. I've got a showing at eleven, closing on another house at one. Oh, and walk-thru right before that—"

Maddie held up her hand. "I get it. I'll be here." No way was she admitting she didn't want to be home alone in the meantime. "Jocelyn should be here in the morning. The others by tomorrow night." She moved closer to her mother. "Why didn't you call and tell me the funeral is scheduled for Sunday? I thought it was going to be on Monday."

Mom put the bottle down. "I did. Check your phone."

Maddie pulled her cell out. One missed call. She must have left it on vibrate. Turning the volume up, she watched the screen. No other texts or Facebook messages. "Look, I want you to take Saturday off. We need you around." She rubbed the smooth surface of the granite. "And there's a lot to do between now and then to get ready for the luncheon after the funeral."

"I...don't know if I can. You know it's busy this time of year."

"Mom," she spoke through gritted teeth. "You have to."

Mom raised her eyebrows. "Madeline." Her own form of threat. "I can't. End of story."

Her hand went to Mom's wrist. "You will."

Her mother grumbled under her breath then squeezed the bridge of her nose. "All right."

That was just a sad excuse. The real reason was that Mom couldn't—no, wouldn't—cope with the loss of her sister.

Mom wrenched her arm free.

Maddie let her go.

"I have to get back to work."

Maddie didn't get a chance to say good-bye as the door slammed.

The woman had a lot of nerve. Maddie glared at the ceiling.

Forget it all. Time to get out. But first find a weapon for defense.

Where should she look? Devin's room would be the most likely place to find something of use. She headed up the stairs and to the end of the hall. In his room, she took great care in not invading his privacy too much. A dulled samurai sword hung from a string. She pulled it down, studied the steel blade, and then re-sheathed it. Another sword rested behind the door. Too bulky and, yet again, dull.

Maddie closed one eye as she opened a desk drawer. Where was his pocket knife collection? She put her hand to her chest. Phew. Right drawer, first try. She looked through the assortment. Even a pink one lay among the masculine knives. She pulled it out. It was small enough to fit in her pocket. She switched it open. Good. Quick sling back. She rubbed her finger across the blade. Very sharp. With it closed, she pushed it into her pocket.

It took her a few minutes to find her purse. She slung the strap over her shoulder and pulled the journal out of the box in the living room.

In the garage, she checked every possible hiding spot she could think of before driving down the driveway. No matter how hard she worked to settle down, jumpiness kept her at full awareness. This stunk. She had a new appreciation for victims of stalkers.

She drove straight to her favorite restaurant with a small dining area and parked as close to the door as possible. Her fingers pried loose from the steering wheel one at a time. She eyed every passerby before she could force herself out of the car. She fingered the knife, checking its exact location to be sure she could grab it fast if need be.

The journal barely fit in her purse. She stuffed it in as carefully as she could and then threw open the restaurant door. A bell tinkled, and the aged owner looked up with a smile.

Maddie took a backseat in the bright orange booth with a Formica tabletop. Ten thirty was a little early for Greek pizza. She breathed in the basil and oregano herb fragrance, so famous in their sauce. But her dry mouth and lack of appetite weren't working with the delicious aromas.

The owner called from the stool by the cash register. "Sorry to hear about your aunt." The sorry sounded like 'sewry.' "Free drinks on me."

"Thanks." She cleared away the moisture in her throat and buried her face in the menu, even though she had it memorized. It didn't deter her that the menu's plastic sleeve had sticky prints on it. The best pizza place was the best. Flaws and all.

The Greek woman smiled. "Your usual?"

She dropped the menu into the holder against the salt and pepper shakers. "Sure."

The woman called the order to the back of the restaurant and returned to the crossword puzzle she had on the counter.

Maddie pulled out the journal. She flipped to the first page. The date read July of the previous year. Nine months ago. Would it be better to start in the back? She twisted her mouth to the side.

A refrigerator hummed somewhere in the open kitchen area. If only the homey comfort of the restaurant would calm the chaos within her. Maddie turned to the last page. The paper at the back of the book was brown, the ink faded. She couldn't make out the last few pages. She kicked the ground a few times. There wasn't a break from it all. Not one break.

When she got to the first legible page, Maddie bent low and ran her finger along the words. Aunt Lonna had beautiful handwriting. It was a list of addresses.

What were they for? Doctor's offices, contacts for the business, old friends? OK, flip the page and go back further.

The previous page was clearer. She went back yet another page to try to get the context. All the words at the end of the page were burned out, making it hard to read.

I met with Marcy today. She wanted all the details on the catering quotes…hate to admit but…haven't had time to get them. She said I signed…so I better get on top of it. I don't need the stress right…

Maddie skimmed through some of it. Apparently, Aunt Lonna had a tiff with one of the other reunion organizers.

There were a few paragraphs about the new business. The trip to Chicago to meet prospective investors had been weighing on Aunt Lonna, and she'd wondered if she was making the right choice.

Maddie looked up. Aunt Lonna must've worked out her hesitation. She was super happy about the outcome of the trip when Maddie'd talked to her just before her return flight.

By the bottom of the page, the burn marks no longer skewed the writing.

She continued to read.

Note to self: Check these addresses. I don't know what he's up to but something's not right. I thought K. had other intentions. Now what?

Who was K.? She skimmed more pages. Nothing else about a K. jumped out. Why couldn't people say what they meant? Why frustrate sneaky readers with code words and such? It's not like any of Aunt Lonna's kids were ever home or would dare read the thing—yet here she was trying to decipher it.

Apprehension snaked up her spine. Was it a dumb move to even think about checking the addresses? Thumbing her fingers on the table, Maddie played with the idea. Her aunt hadn't seemed afraid of looking into them, so should she be? Could the stalker have ties to the addresses, or was it something unrelated? Were they actually tied to some type of sabotage of the reunion?

The addresses couldn't wait. With a thump, she sat back against the booth seat. She should call Joze. Even if he hated her right now. But hadn't she just been telling herself she wouldn't ask him for help under any circumstances? Anyway, he was probably at work. And they weren't exactly on speaking terms after the God conversation. Not after she shoved him out the door.

Without another thought, Maddie yanked her phone out and searched his number. Ten seconds later, staring at it hadn't solidified a decision whether to call him or not. She shook her head and hit the green phone symbol and scrunched her eyes closed. It was better to apologize and be safe then go alone.

Was this conversation going to have to come with an apology? She winced. When it went to voice mail, Maddie didn't know if she should be relieved or not. "Hey, Joze. This is Maddie. Uh, you probably figured that out. Um, I found some addresses in the journal. I'm going to check them out." She rattled off the first one. "I thought you might want to come, but you must be at work or something." She bit her lip. "So I'm headed to one of them. Just wanted you to know. I'll be careful."

Her shoulders sank almost to the tabletop as she hung up. Maddie had to do this for Aunt Lonna.

The owner rounded the counter carrying Maddie's pizza on a metal cooking sheet. Maddie raised her forefinger. "Can you make it to go?"

The woman waved. "No prob."

Maddie whisked the box out of the woman's hand and thanked her again a couple minutes later. At her car, Maddie surveyed the street and parking lot and hurried to lock her doors.

She put the first address in her phone. A Hartford address. Her GPS zoomed to the location. She squirmed. Danger at home. Possible danger scouting out the addresses. Give or take, it didn't matter which one she chose. But at home she was a sitting duck. Hartford was a good twenty-five minutes away. She checked the time.

She put in the other two addresses. One was semi-local. The other one was also in Hartford. Might as well drive into the city. She might even have time to see both locations. What about waiting for Joze to call back? But if he was working, he could be gone all day.

Maddie flew down Route 384. Traffic was light for the time of day. The gloom must be keeping people in. She searched for any vehicles that could be following her. Too many were the same color or similar make. How would she know? There didn't seem to be a pattern to any of them. A tow truck and ambulance worked their way west also.

The GPS talked to her the whole way. Stay in the left two lanes. Move to the right lane. Exit in one point two miles. Stay on 84 West.

Traffic slowed as she entered the city. Victorian houses began to look more and more dingy. Peeling paint became the norm. Her shoulders went up with each passing street crossing.

Maddie glanced down to see if her doors were locked. The button was fully depressed. She sighed and looked from left to right.

The trash began to build up on the sidewalks and down the streets that crumbled away from the main roadway.

Then a few drops of rain splotched on her

windshield.

The next four street corners were covered by a motley crew of people hurrying to their destinations under the gray skies.

The light turned green. Maddie put her foot on the accelerator, eyes trained on one of the men. A loud bang rang from the front of her car and she stomped the brake. She looked out the windshield into the squinted eyes of a woman, her hair standing straight up four inches, her cardigan holey and from the seventies. The woman pushed a bike across the street, its basket full with a trash bag. Maddie shivered and ran a hand through her hair.

Just as she pushed the accelerator again, the GPS seemed to shout. "In point two miles, turn right at the next intersection. The destination will be on your right. 164 Draper Street."

This was not a bad idea; it was the worst. Maddie didn't dare stop when she made the turn, but she slowed to a crawl. Trash pickup day must be today. Big, ugly green cans were so full, they couldn't possibly be lifted and dumped into the compactor when it came by.

"You have reached your destination." She sucked in a breath. Yikes.

A three-story Victorian in three shades of neon paint glowered down at her. Smoke billowed from the chimney running up its side. Three levels of porches sagged across the front.

She pulled to the curb and stopped, grasping the steering wheel for dear life. Maddie hunched down to get a better look. Someone moved from the top porch back into the house.

She pressed her purse to her chest as she scanned

the area. The other houses were more tired than run down, not like the neon mess in front of her.

With shaking hands, Maddie put her phone in her left pocket and stepped out of the car. Music blared from somewhere across the street.

An old lady, at least in her eighties, sat forward from a decrepit couch on the porch next door. She stuck her finger in her mouth and pried at something, never taking her eyes off Maddie. Should Maddie wave? She drew herself up to her full five-foot four inches. She put her fingers up in a kind of wave. The woman stopped picking her teeth but didn't return the gesture.

Maddie turned back. What shade of green would you call the second level? And the Purple on the bottom? Grape.

Someone was on the third-floor porch again. A man with unkempt hair and an oil-stained T-shirt leaned over and watched her, a cigarette in his hand. She hurried up the broken walk.

Five apartment numbers graced the frame of the door. The journal had said apartment 3D. Maddie held her breath and walked through the front door that hung on one hinge. Something scurried away. Please let it be a Chihuahua.

The guy from the third floor darted down the stairs and skipped the last couple steps. "Hello." He walked right up to her. "You need somethin'?"

She backed to the wall, hand going to her pocket. "I...I—"

He placed a hand on the wall by her right shoulder and took a long look at her physique.

Why had she been so dumb as to come alone? She begged the bile in her esophagus to stay down.

Vomiting all over this guy would probably bring her death quicker. Keep control. Don't pass out. Todd's face shimmered before her eyes.

She gulped a breath. "Please back away. Now." Not a convincing tone. "I mean it."

He moved closer not further away, and breathed his dank breath on her.

"I was wondering if anyone here had seen a woman." Her voice quivered. "My aunt." She took a shallow breath. "I have a picture. I...can show you."

He blinked. "Someone like you comin' up in here alone? I don' know about that."

He looked away. Maddie bolted to the left and pulled the knife out of her pocket. It wouldn't flick open as it had at her house.

He returned his dull eyes to her. "Where's your purse?" He scuffled his feet and looked around. "Hand it over."

Banging and screeching shuttered through the house. Maddie dared not turn to look at the open door on the far end of the hall from where the sound emanated.

"Yo, George, who ya talkin' to?" The rough voice of a woman stopped his movements. He recoiled, shoulders back. The innocent look on his wide face must not have worked. "Let me talk to the lady."

Maddie turned enough to keep him in her sights but also to see who was talking. A woman, about ready to burst with child, pushed a lopsided stroller to the side of the hall. The squealing and banging ceased. "Hey, can I help you?"

Maddie shoved the knife back into her pocket. "I don't mean to bother you but, I'm looking for—" If she said 'information', everyone might take her for the law and run. "I wondered if you'd ever seen this woman before." She pulled up her photo gallery on her phone and clicked on Aunt Lonna's picture.

The soon-to-be mom grasped the phone. Maddie couldn't hold onto it as she moved away with it. "Nope. Don't recognize her. Is she with the Ladies Benevolent Fund? They were here tryin' to give stuff to Eddie in 2B."

"Um, no." Maddie followed the lady to the back where she squinted at the picture in the light of the doorway. She breathed in fresher air—a little less men's locker room fresh.

"Follow me. Eddie might know."

For being so pregnant, the woman took the stairs like an athlete. Maddie hurried to keep up. She almost touched the thick, carved railing but noted the grime encasing it. At the second floor, the woman barreled down the hall. "Hey, Eddie. Got a question for you."

The walls must be as thin as paper. He opened his door and peeked out. "Whatta you want, Beth?"

She plunged the phone through the opening. Maddie fought an urge to wrestle it away as it passed to Eddie. She clutched her hands together.

"Nah." His smoke-stained fingers, caked in something black, held her phone. Maddie resisted a gag.

Beth pilfered the phone from him so fast he almost dropped it in the exchange.

Her guide turned down the hall and headed back the way they came. She dropped Maddie's cell into her hand. "RoRo might know about your lady. He's not here." She winked. "Business and all this time o' day."

Maddie let the phone fall into her purse and gulped. What now? Raised voices traveled up the stairs. She fished out a new business card. "Here. Could you call me if you see RoRo again? I'm in a real bind. I need to talk to him."

Again, the raised voice. She turned toward it. There was something familiar. She peered down the stairwell and then gave a fake smile to Beth. "Gotta go. Thanks again."

"Sure." Beth put the card down her shirt.

Joze? No. Way.

He popped his head around the turn in the stair. "Madeline Clare. Come here—please."

Should she be exuberant he was there to help her get past the pervert at the front door?

Beth let her go. "Watch the one step. It's weak on the far side."

What side would that be? Maddie took the center the whole way down.

Joze looked like a bull ready to charge a red flag. Steam seemed to pour out his nostrils. "Come on."

He tried to help her out of the house but she balked. "Hey. Stop."

It took him a second to let her move of her own accord. Then he plowed down the walk until they were at her car. "Get in." He eyed the neighboring houses. "Now, please."

At least he hadn't forgotten his manners. Maddie hit *unlock* on the key fob and climbed in.

"Follow me."

Where'd he come from? She looked around. An ambulance idled three houses down. His ambulance?

As fast as she could, she flipped a U-turn and got back on Route 84 right behind the ambulance.

The further they went, the more her blood boiled. What choice did he think she had? She had to investigate, or the stalking—or worse—would never end.

Was he on his lunch break? How else could he drive out of his jurisdiction?

As they crossed a bridge, trees lined the sidewalk at the other end. The buildings glowed cleaner and whiter.

Joze pulled into a strip mall and flew out of the driver seat.

Her car was barely in park when he yanked her door open. "Are you OK?" He checked her arm. "Did he hurt you?" His wide eyes grazed over her face. "No wounds?"

How could she still be mad at him?

14

Of all the crazy schemes, why'd Maddie have to pick the most dangerous one of all? Joze slammed the car door behind Maddie. Good thing he'd noticed her message right after his last emergency call a couple miles down one of the highways nearby. Because of the sheer number of victims, ambulances had been called in from the county on a three-car accident with multiple critically injured persons. And his buddies were willing to go along with him to follow her since they were all starving and ready for a quick bite to eat. "What're you doing out here?" He grabbed his head with both hands. "That place houses gang members?"

She braced against her car, hands up and close enough to touch his abdomen. "Wait a minute."

He breathed, skin tingling even though she hadn't laid a hand on him. Maddie drove him crazy in more ways than one. He managed to muster some control. "Look, let's go sit down and talk."

"I...have a pizza in my car."

"I'm paying. Come on." Before he killed her in public.

His two friends and co-workers ogled her from the front seat of the ambulance as they walked. Then they got out of the vehicle. "Hey."

He stopped. "Maddie, you remember Jim? That's Tom."

She kept walking but glanced back. "Hi."

He waved them on and caught up to her. The other EMTs found a booth of their own but continued to watch Joze as he let her pick the booth she wanted. He mouthed, "Stop," but they only smirked and stared more. He'd have to talk to them later.

She was smart enough to take a seat at the rear, knowing he was about to start yelling at her.

Joze prayed hard. "Please God, let me keep my cool." He pulled off a neutral tone even though he wanted to yell through the rafters. "Can you tell me why you were out there?"

She rested her head against the back wall. "I found some addresses in the journal. There's no difference between sitting at home waiting for the bad man to get me and doing a little investigating." Then she folded her arms. "So don't even think you're going to stop me."

Calm down. "And you went to one of them to do what?"

"To see if they knew my aunt." She huffed.

"Listen. You're acting crazy—" He closed his eyes a moment and then enunciated each word. "Sorry. You're taking unnecessary risks."

Maddie crumbled a little. "Yeah," She pinched her face tight, "It wasn't very smart to go it alone."

His heart melted a little more. She wasn't the same unreasonable Maddie he knew from their college days. He crossed his own arms. But she had kicked him out earlier. "I'm not going away."

"Even if I paid you?" She couldn't hide a smirk.

He snorted. "No matter what."

She stopped and quirked her mouth. "Well, you did leave when I kicked you out."

He sat forward. "I needed a break."

Maddie lowered her gaze. "You won't run off again even if you don't believe me about Todd?"

She had him there. "You said even your mom didn't believe you. But let's stay in the present."

She forced her way off the seat and pushed her blond hair out of her face. "I can't believe—"

"I'm sorry." He reached for her hand before she could pass. He had a way with words like a bull in a china shop. God help him, please. "That was not fair."

She stopped, her lips one thin line.

He lowered his voice. "Please sit down. I won't mention it again."

She actually sat. His stomach slowed its churning.

They ordered drinks and sandwiches.

Joze steepled his hands. "You got a chance to read some of the journal. Did you find a name for your stalker? Because that was my biggest fear…when I saw you going into downtown Hartford."

"No. Only the addresses, like I said before."

Oh, yeah. "Your aunt didn't let on that she was afraid of any particular person?"

She played with her sleeve. "Only someone she called K."

"Like the woman's name Kay?"

"No. The letter K. I don't know if it's a woman or a man."

He sipped his drink as they sat in silence. Then he glanced back at his buddies. They were happy with the sandwiches in front of them and not staring down Joze and Maddie anymore.

He turned back. Was she holding back information? They had to call a truce. Now. And it had to involve dropping the past. "I want to start all over,

Maddie. We need each other."

She gaped at him.

He held up a hand. "Wait. Hear me out. I have the connections. You have the journal. Let's do this together." Lord help him. "Please. If you want to go to the rough side of town, wait for me. I know some of the people out there." He caught her eye. "Church ministry. Enough said."

"Fine, but I'm making the decisions."

Could he agree to that term? "As long as it doesn't involve gang members."

She gave a short laugh. Good, the mood was lightening. "Do you know who RoRo is?"

He was back to full alert. "What does he have to do with this? I've heard of him. Stay away from him. He's part of a gang, and he's suspected of human trafficking."

"Well, I'll get myself a gun. No worries."

He squeezed his plastic cup hard enough to make the tips of his fingers turn white. Was she serious? "Your pretty face is exactly what he's looking for. And a little gun won't stop a whole gang if they come after you. I'm not kidding when I say don't ever talk to him."

She grimaced and narrowed her eyes but for once didn't respond.

Why try to fix the things flying out of his mouth? It was no use.

She took a bite of her sandwich. She did seem different—more…something. And she'd grown more beautiful in the passing years than he thought possible. With all his promises and deals, did he think he'd manage to keep his distance and move on when the situation was resolved?

Not likely. Even if he wanted to.

15

The restaurant served a steady flow of customers as Joze and Maddie sat in the silence of a truce. Maddie fished the pickle off her plate and took a bite. Tangy. Kind of like Joze. *No, no. Don't fall for his charms.* She'd work with him but only because she couldn't be alone right now. And he had a point. Connections made things easier.

She finished off the pickle, watching Joze the whole time. She'd never known him to stay silent so long.

"I have…some things to do." She'd better tell him and hope he didn't get upset all over again. "—Like two more addresses to check. I'm sure you have to get back to work, but…"

He wiped his mouth and eyed her. "I was off for the day, but the crew needed a little support. . So I thought I'd tag along and help the guys. And they were kind enough to drive me on a nice, high-speed chase to find you in return."

"Hey." She threw her napkin across the table. "You shouldn't speed."

He laughed, picked up the napkin, and dropped it on his empty plate. "Right. If you don't mind giving me a ride to my car, I can let the guys head back to Anby, and I'll go with you."

The waitress dropped their check on the table. Joze

pulled out his wallet.

Maddie grabbed the thin paper. "I've got this."

"I said I'd buy you lunch, remember?"

She slowly relinquished it.

She glanced to the other EMTs. "Um, sure."

He narrowed his eyes and set some bills on top of the check. "Now what's the plan?"

She dropped her shoulders and looked to the ceiling. "The security place isn't due to the house until two, so we have enough time to check the second address. It's here in Hartford." He opened his mouth wide to say something, but she stopped him. "Cool it. It's not on the bad side of town—well, not really—I don't think."

"Fine. Let's go."

She rolled her eyes in mock agitation. "If you must."

He moved out of the booth and held his index finger up to ask her to wait. After talking to his buddies, they waved at her and ambled out of the restaurant.

Joze took slow steps back to her. "Can I see the address?"

She pursed her lips. Then she gave up and took out the journal. Maddie opened it and riffled through until she found the right page. "Here."

He took it and read it out loud. "I think I know where that is."

"GPS knows where everything is." Scooting out, she took the book from him. "Come on."

On the road, they got back on the highway and headed south.

Joze pressed his arm against the side of the door frame. "What do you think your aunt had to do with

RoRo? He's not the kind of guy innocent old ladies look up."

"Don't know." Maddie wished she could even take a guess. It became more and more obvious that she didn't know Aunt Lonna at all anymore. Or was it more that the grown-up aunt was really always a different person?

"You never knew of any drug abuse or anything of that nature?"

Maddie wanted to smack him. She gulped in a breath. "Of course not." There weren't any signs of such a thing. "Look, RoRo is a surprise to me as much as you, but drugs wouldn't have anything to do with Aunt Lonna. She was a naturalist through and through. She'd never put that stuff in her body."

He shrugged. "Well, why else would she be seeking a gang leader? And what do you know about this other address? Did you find anything in the diary to give some clues?"

"Nope."

They pulled up to a brick six-story building fifteen minutes later. Maddie glanced out the window. "Looks like some type of business park."

They both got out and stopped in front of the car.

Joze crossed his arms. "The hospital's right down the street a block. This looks like doctors' offices."

Maddie shielded her eyes from the sun. "It does. Come on. let's go check them out."

How long would it take to go office to office?

Joze put a hand to her arm. "You know you can't go flashing around a picture of your aunt. Patient confidentiality. No one'll talk to you."

It was worth a try. Maddie headed to the main entrance. But Joze would know. He worked in the medical field. "Fine, but we can take a look."

The posh gray marble floors and mahogany doors that reached to the ceiling gave the bottom floor an air of opulence and light. Joze guided her to a plaque on the wall. "Take a picture with your phone. Then we can refer back to it later."

Good thinking. She pulled it out and snapped a few. Cardiologists, ENTs, a pediatrician or two, and a general surgeon's office covered every floor. Maddie frowned as she ran her finger down the list. Had Aunt Lonna been sick? Why would that be on the list of places to check?

Nothing made any sense. "I don't get it."

"You want to go to each floor?"

"Might as well, since we're here." She marched from one end of the hall to the other.

At the elevators, they went up to each floor. All identical to the bottom one. She threw up her hands. "This isn't doing any good. Not when we have no clue what this building meant to my aunt."

Joze pressed the button to head back down to the first level. They stepped in, the only other occupant a man in a white coat.

Maddie nodded a hello to him. He gave a tight-lipped response and pushed the button to the fifth floor. When the elevator trembled to a stop and the doors opened, he glanced back at them and walked away at a brisk pace.

Typical. "Doctors."

Joze pressed the button to close the door. He moved closer to her. She eyed him. All the funny little quirky things about him played through her mind. How she'd loved his sense of humor. And the way he'd always looked out for her at college—kind of like he did now—made her want to stop pushing him away. The elevator dropped, sending her stomach into a spin. She braced herself against his arm, and he reached out and steadied her. Why did her heart want to jump back into the old rhythm of desire for him? She forced down the familiar tingle of his closeness. Don't love him again. He'd never fit into her world again. Not if he couldn't believe her. And letting the past go wasn't the same thing as believing her.

Maddie moved a few inches away until her shoulder bumped the black marble wall.

The elevator jerked to a stop. Her arms flailed, of their own accord, out to Joze. Why couldn't she get her body to agree with her mind? He wrapped an arm around her shoulder as the lights flickered out. "What's going on?"

"Hold still. It's only a hiccup in the system, I'm sure."

She couldn't stop from moving into his embrace. A shiver traveled through her. Too many heart-pumping, sheer-terror moments of the last twenty-four hours passed through her mind.

When the lights didn't come on and the machine didn't start to descend in a normal everyday way, Maddie fought to take a breath and urged her heart to keep its normal rhythm. "Joze…"

He dropped one of his hands. "It's fine. This happens now and then. Let me get to the buttons."

As he released her, Maddie forced her arms to her side. Stop being ridiculous. Stop letting fear work into every muscle. Who even knew they were there?

Then a screech and a crack sent the elevator plummeting down.

Maddie couldn't keep her balance. She fell to the

floor with a yelp.

Joze's arms were back around her, hoisting her up. He pulled her to the button panel. With a thump, he hit the emergency button. In a split second, the elevator jolted to a stop.

Maddie screamed and squeezed her eyes closed.

The lights came back on.

The doors opened as if nothing had happened.

The flesh of Joze's skin under her nails dimpled, and red marks popped up. She released him so fast she almost fell out of the elevator. *Get out. Get out.* "Sorry."

Her shoes smacked onto the marble tiles, safe on the first floor.

Joze rewrapped his arms around her, his breath coming out in ragged bursts.

They both sagged against the wall to catch their breath. Maddie twisted her head side to side at the people heading down the hall. "What just happened? That could've been a fluke event, right?"

A couple moved to the elevator. Maddie and Joze both yelled, "Stop."

The couple pulled back and frowned.

With his hand blocking their entrance, Joze stood up straight. "It's broken. We almost went through the basement floor."

The man took three steps back and frowned. "Maybe we'll take the stairs."

Joze nodded and caught his breath as they hurried away. "I can't let anyone fall in that elevator. I just can't. I promise I'll be right back.. I better get someone to put up an 'out of service' sign. You stay here and keep anyone from getting on it."

No, no, no. *Don't leave me here.* Maddie watched him disappear. It could not be a coincidence that the elevator had almost killed them. That meant the stalker could be here. She pressed her back to the wall, hands splayed on the cool surface of the wall.

Three separate people tried to climb on.

"No. This one is out of service." She wasn't about to tell them they almost died like Joze had told the first couple. Who knew what shape the other elevator was in either? "You might want to take the stairs."

Most of them took her advice except one gray-haired man who waved off her comment. She watched the numbers change in a slow ascent. It stopped as it should.

She breathed a sigh. It was only their elevator that was malfunctioning.

She scanned the people coming and going. No familiar faces.

The working elevator dinged beside her, making her jump and yelp.

Someone slid out when the doors opened. A woman in a navy business suit, with a wheeled bag trailing behind her.

The woman ignored her and strode to the lobby and out the doors. She didn't have killer written on her.

When a workman in jeans and a black uniform shirt passed the hall, she leaned out to watch him go. Interesting. But when he pivoted on his heel and ogled her, Maddie pressed back against the wall, bumping her head. Where was Joze? She clenched the top of her collar, stifled by it. It took thought to breathe in and out. And to not look like she was about to have a panic attack.

The man sauntered closer to the elevators.

Should she leap in the other elevator and get out

of there? But what about Joze?

She gulped.

He slid his fingers into the corners of his jeans pockets. "You the one looking for help?"

"I—"

Joze rounded the corner then stopped. "Sir, it's the first one."

Joze moved to her and took her hand. Maddie squeezed back. "I'm fine."

Joze explained to the maintenance man what had happened in the elevator, then pulled her away. She didn't resist. When he got her out the main doors, Joze steered her to the edge of some tall bushes. "Did you see someone familiar?"

She checked their surroundings. In any other situation, it would seem like a superior clandestine location. Maddie did a double take. Why'd her mind go to that thought? She shook it off and pulled her hand out of his. "Um, no."

He gazed down at his empty palm. "You know, the chances of that being caused by someone are so slim...but still I don't want to leave you alone."

She brushed the hair off her shoulder and bit her bottom lip. What if she didn't want him to leave her alone once the bad guy was caught either?

16

The draw to Maddie wasn't any good for Joze. He dropped his hand. If only she'd left her soft fingers entwined in his. He struggled to focus on the people coming and going down the sidewalk and then studied the enclosure of bushes. A good place to remain unseen. Had the unknown subject been here when they'd arrived and watched them enter the building? "If this situation is any sign, our unknown suspect has to work at this building. It would explain why the address was in the journal too."

Maddie shifted from foot to foot. "I don't know. What if it's a fluke thing? Not an intentional breakdown of the elevator? Could he have followed us again?"

"Anything's possible, but it's not likely. I had my eye on the road the whole time. I didn't see the same vehicle making turns with us." He started to pace. "Hmm." He looked up at the building. All the windows stared down at him. "We should get out of here. If he's here right now, you need to be somewhere safe. And it wouldn't hurt to call the police and report it just in case."

She checked the time on her phone. "I have to be home in an hour. And later tonight, all my cousins will be there. I can't leave them alone with this crazy stuff happening."

What were the chances Mrs. Clare would let him stay at the house through the night? Not great. "Come on."

Maddie pulled onto the road, and he kept his eyes peeled behind them.

She flipped her turn signal on and scooted between two cars. "I think we should call the police and report this."

Was the black SUV in the left lane following them? He strained to watch as it fell back a car length. "What could we tell them? We don't know for sure what happened."

"True." She stopped at a light in the right turn lane.

The man behind the wheel never looked in their direction but drove through the main green light. Drumming a beat against his leg, Joze watched him pass and eased back.

It didn't take long to get to Anby, where Joze directed her to his parked car. The whole trip may've been uneventful, but he couldn't shake the tension pulling at his muscles. "I'll follow you, OK?"

When he pulled into her drive, the security team sat in their van on the curb. He got out and waited for her to come through the garage.

Two men converged on the porch, a tool bag and clipboard in their hands. They got to work planning out the installation and counting how many sensors to use. Then Maddie signed some forms and gave them reign to do what they needed to do. Sassie must've already worked out the general package she wanted and sent them specs on the house. What a relief they could come on such short notice.

It took Joze a minute to stop staring at them as

they headed to the back door. They didn't need him assessing their every move. He reached out to Maddie. "Let's read the journal. I want to know everything I can about this stalker."

She set her purse on the desk in the library. "Do you think he chased my aunt this much too?"

"Wouldn't your mom have known if it'd been this serious? They did share this house."

Maddie lowered herself into the desk chair and put her head in her hands. "My mom isn't home a lot."

And she was very self-involved. Joze kept the comment to himself. His fingers itched to take the book from Maddie. With the slowest of movements, she took it out, stared at the cover, and then sighed.

Come on, Maddie. What was she waiting for? "You want me to read it?" He knew the answer, but it was worth a shot. He put his hand out. "Please."

"Drag that chair over here. We'll look at it together."

He didn't have to be told twice. Lifting the chair over the desk, Joze deposited it as close to hers as he could get and sat.

Maddie pushed one of her sleeves up and told him how many months the journal covered. "Where should we start? The beginning or what?"

"We'll have to do a lot of backtracking if we don't."

She flipped to the first page. Several weeks of information on what went into trying to establish the new soap business seemed to be all Lonna Selby was worried about. Kids at college. Mrs. Clare not ever home. Nothing significant.

As Maddie eased back in her chair she turned the page. "November ninth." She rubbed her eyes. "She started working with her classmates on the upcoming reunion."

It was just too tempting to take the book. He reached for it, and she released it without a comment. Surprise. She went without a fight? "Want me to read it to you?"

"Sure."

Joze creased the page. "OK." He scanned a few lines. "She says she started a list of classmates and created a social media page for the reunion."

He read her the next several entries and then stopped. "Look." He held it up for her to see. "She met someone from her class. She says she hopes to see him again."

They both stared at each other. This had to be significant. "So she was dating someone?"

Keep reading. They had to be getting to vital clues. "She says, 'We went out tonight. Had the best time. I can't remember when the last time was that I've been out that late with a man. He didn't get me flowers or anything. That must be a bygone thing. But still, he's charming.'" He set the book in his lap. "She never mentioned any of this?"

"Maybe it was short-lived. I don't know."

He picked it back up and began to read. As he turned the page, the corner crumbled a little, leaving black soot on his jeans. *Uh-oh, better be careful or she'll snatch it back.* He smoothed the fine paper with gentle fingers.

One of the technicians tapped on the library door. "Ma'am, we're almost finished. But, there are a few questions we wanted to clear with you."

Joze stretched forward to watch her leave and then thumbed through the book. If she caught him reading it without her there, would it start a world war? He took one more look at the hall. Where oh where was the information they really needed?

Scanning fast, he ran his finger down each page and kept an eye on the door. More soap stuff and more laments about being home alone a lot. OK, no more boyfriend? His finger fell on the letter K again.

Maddie hurried into the room, stopped at the desk, and thumped the table. He startled. She didn't glance at him. Maybe she hadn't noticed him digging through the pages for information. He tried to look innocent.

With exasperation, she raked a hand through her hair. "Who knew those things were so complicated? I hope I don't forget all that stuff they told me."

"Did they give you a manual? We'll figure it out as long as we have one." How hard could it be?

"Yeah."

He got up and stretched. "They left?"

She nodded. "See, now I'm safe. You don't have to worry about me anymore."

How could he possibly stop worrying about her now? This had gone from nothing to complicated in no time. "Yeah, but I don't want to leave you anyway." Did that sound desperate? He wasn't going for desperate. "What if the police can't get here in time?" That came out better. Bet she hadn't considered that scenario. "And then he's got you."

She frowned and fell into her seat. "I guess it's possible but—"

Come on Maddie, let me stay. He could sit out in his car and watch the place if she said no.

And just like that she gave him a determined look, eyebrow arched. "I have got to get some homework done. Thanks for all that you've done." It sounded like he was getting the boot. "It's been good seeing you again."

Yep.

She stood and went to the library door.

"Why won't you listen to me?" He set the book on the desk and stood. "I'm not trying to do anything but help."

Maddie pursed her lips. "I know. I really appreciate it too."

His fists balled at his sides. Fine. She wanted to take her chances? Go for it. "You have my number."

This woman made him nuts. Granted, not always in a bad way. He couldn't deny how much he longed for the days when they were so close and had so much in common. A time when they were inseparable. Joze paced back and forth in front of his car. It took willpower not to kick the brand-new after-market tires he'd installed a few months back. How did she think she'd fend off a driven stalker? Didn't she know that in the real world, women like her got hurt and even died because they didn't take the situation seriously enough? He'd seen it on his watch. And he wasn't going to let her be the next victim in his town.

With determination, Joze sat in his car and rolled the window down. Time to do it his way.

17

Why'd Joze have to make a big deal about the security system and the police? Every sound from the ice machine kicking on, every movement or passing vehicle made her jerk to attention. For the fourth time, she tried to concentrate on her laptop screen.

It didn't make sense to send Joze away. She chewed her lip. He offered. She should've accepted. But it would mean she'd have to stave off feelings she'd put to death a long time ago. And it got harder with each passing hour. Which made no sense. She'd left him four years ago. Done. No going back. But now she couldn't deny how much having him around made her want him again. Did he still care for her too? Yet the past couldn't be forgotten.

Wasn't safety more important right now, though? And Joze hadn't made a move on her yet. He'd been helpful and protective. And hadn't she seen something in his eyes more akin to love than indifference? At the time she ignored it, but looking back Maddie had to admit it was there.

She raked cold fingers through her hair and surveyed the yard outside the window.

Her cell phone rang, and she checked the screen. Cousin Aster. She'd spent the day driving from New York to get home. "Hey, it's me. Are you almost here?"

Aster's clear voice sounded through the phone. "I

should be home in less than an hour."

"Great." She didn't need Joze after all. "Be safe."

They hung up.

Devin, the oldest of Aunt Lonna's children would be home a few hours from now. Who'd dare break in with a house full of people?

Maddie dropped the device and got up to check the alarm system one more time. Dinner would be a good idea to make. She dug in the fridge and pulled out some ground beef. How about lasagna? It was her favorite meal to cook. She riffled through the cabinets. Was there sauce and noodles and cheese?

After her search, everything but spinach sat on the countertop. Oh well, it would still be good without it. She started the water for the noodles, put the meat in a pan to fry, and picked up a wooden spoon.

She plunged the spoon into the sauce and stirred. The whole time, Maddie couldn't shake the sense of eyes watching her every move. Sheer curtains in the side window didn't help block the view. At least there were solid blinds on the door window and the one over the sink.

Maddie stopped herself from turning toward the window. Should she get a blanket from the closet and throw it over the curtain rod?

She set down the wooden spoon and headed straight to the closet. Why keep suffering?

With the job done, she stood back and regarded it. Finally, she could stop worrying that her own personal stalker was out there, peeking in.

With the last layer of cheese in place, Maddie picked up the pan to put it in the oven.

A beeping screamed through the house. She grasped the pan, heart in her throat. The door knob turned. She dropped the pan and it clattered on the counter.

Aster entered through the back door, fumbling with something. "What's that horrid sound?"

Maddie grasped her chest. She sucked in a breath and then hurried to the alarm wall mount. What code word had she picked? She hit the silence button and put the password in. It quieted a moment later. "You scared me to death."

A suitcase dropped out of Aster's hands to the tiled floor. "And that thing scared me. Since when did Aunt Sassie need a security system? She won't even lock the doors when she's at work."

How could she avoid the interrogation? She sputtered but couldn't find the right lie. "You know, times are different. I convinced her it would be good to have one." That sounded weak. "You never know what could happen."

Aster set the rest of her things down and ran to hug Maddie. "I missed you. It smells good in here. Please tell me that's your lasagna."

"It is." She relished the hug. "I want to hear all about college in New York."

Her cousin pulled away. "I'll be right back. Potty break."

Maddie picked up the pan again and deposited it in the oven. Twenty minutes would do.

She moved her cousin's things to the bottom of the stairs. Could she convince Aster they should bunk in the same room tonight? Somehow, she didn't think it would go over too well since they hadn't done so in over ten years.

That's right, Devin would be home tonight too. She let her chin fall to her chest as she leaned against the stair railing. Too much stress was making her sick. Her stomach rumbled with acid.

It was going to be OK, wasn't it? If only she could call on God as she had as a child. But He would never answer her, not after she'd decided to forget His existence. Maybe He'd sent the present trouble. Why would He get her out of it, even if she wanted to believe in prayer again?

Aster practically skipped toward her. She pushed her glasses up on her nose, and her blue eyes sparkled. "Hey." Her hand was warm on Maddie's shoulder. "What's going on?"

Everything. "Nothing." She shifted her focus. "I just can't believe what's happened to Aunt Lonna. I never thought we'd be here dealing with this. Not right now."

Aster didn't hold back the tears the way Maddie did. Maddie took her cousin in her arms and rubbed her back the way she had when they were kids and Aster was upset or hurt. Aster's soft blond curls blocked her vision for a moment.

"You've always been like a little mama to us, Maddie. Thank you."

Maddie couldn't stave off the stinging in her eyes. "You're welcome." She pulled away. "I better check the lasagna."

Tangy spaghetti sauce and basil aromas filled the air. At least the normalcy of a meal with family could keep the creeps out of her mind for a while.

The shrieking alarm split through the room again. Good thing the pan wasn't in her hand yet. Maddie hopped up.

Mom.

She ran to reenter the code again.

Sassie set her briefcase down. "I see they came."

When was the last time Mom had bothered to come home so early? "I wasn't expecting you 'til late."

Mom kicked her shoes across the floor. "You made your lasagna?"

"Uh-huh. Except it's missing the spinach." Maddie tilted her head and studied her mom. "How was work?"

"Good. Busy." She stood from peering in the stove. "I do hear you, ya know."

Better not get into that discussion in front of Aster. "Thanks, Mom. Want to eat in the dining room?"

Mom smiled. "That would be nice. Let me change."

Maddie and Aster set the long oak table in the beige and cream room. Aster put a fork at each setting. "When's Devin going to be here? He didn't make it home for Christmas. I miss him."

He never did maintain contact well. "He should be home by nine tonight."

Mom came back wearing yoga pants and a cotton T-shirt. "I'll get the glasses."

With fingers crossed, the meal had a slight chance of happening with minimal tension. Maddie took the pan out and brought it to the table.

The doorbell sang a song from the front foyer. Who could that be? Maddie dropped the napkin onto the table and hurried out of her chair. "I'll get it."

Aster beat her to the dining room doorway. "Let me. You cooked. Relax."

She opened and shut her mouth. What if—?

The alarm system beeped. Good, her cousin remembered to disarm it.

Joze's voice carried down the hall. "It's good to see

you again."

As the voices drew closer, Aster giggled. "Yeah. I didn't know you were back."

Maddie put her hand to her forehead. What was he doing here? Great. Mom and he would be the death of the meal for sure. She stood and worked to stabilize the shrill in her voice. "Hey, Joze."

Mom's eyes grew big, but her gaze stayed on the cheesy mess on her plate. "Joseph."

Take Mom's side or Joze's?

Mom would disappear in her work. Joze seemed to be there for good. He would stick around in case she needed him. Tonight at least.

"I'll get you a plate." The tone in Mom's voice could break glass.

With his thumbs hooked in the back pockets of his jeans, Joze remained outside the dining room as if he knew his intrusion wasn't OK. "Sorry to interrupt. But thanks."

Should she ask why he'd showed up so unexpectedly? Maybe not in front of the family.

Glass, silverware, and plate in hand, Maddie returned to the dining room. He started to speak but she gave him a warning look, and he shut up.

The lasagna didn't taste as good with the strain filtering around the room. Maddie cleared her throat. "Anyone want some ice cream? I can get it out to thaw."

Joze shot her a questioning glance.

She returned it with a wide-eyed stare and mouthed, "We'll talk later."

He pressed his lips together.

Aster prattled on about college life and her new boyfriend. Either she didn't notice the cold stares from

Mom or she was refusing to acknowledge them. Maddie wasn't sure.

Joze kept up with Aster's fast New York talk she'd adopted. At least it kept Maddie from having to steer the conversation to safe ground the whole time.

It was good to see Aster so sure and happy. Yet sadness tinged her eyes the entire meal.

Devin arrived as Maddie brought the ice cream to the table. "What are you doing home already?"

He squeezed her tight, his duffel bag smacking her right arm. "I got an earlier flight. I couldn't take another minute of speech class."

She breathed in his earthy cologne. "I'm so glad you're here."

When he released her, she studied his stubbled jawline that was wider than she remembered. He lifted the corner of his mouth. "And not crashing onto the tarmac?"

He always had a way with words. Not the right way. Maddie grimaced. "Devin."

"What?" He hugged Mom. "Insensitive, I get it. Sorry."

18

Joze eyed Maddie's cousin, Devin, stood, and put out his hand. Two cousins home, one left to arrive. "Good to see you."

Devin dropped his duffel bag on the Oriental rug and shook his hand. "Joze, right?"

He nodded. Had he been that memorable?

"Are we having a party or what?"

It seemed more like a war waging right under the surface of conversation. "If you want to call it that."

Maddie and Aster served Devin a huge helping of dinner. The whole time, he talked with his mouth full.

More than once Joze had to force himself to pay attention to the new bout of chat around the table. At least Mrs. Clare had stopped giving him the stink-eye. He studied Maddie as much as he could. She steered all conversation clear of the past couple days. Why? She had mentioned she wanted to keep a tight wrap on it, but he didn't like it one bit.

Devin spread his hand on the table. "Joze, you're a paramedic?"

What? He'd missed something. "An EMT."

"Cool. I have my degree in nursing, but I work for an insurance company."

All the eyes looking back at him were blue. Definitely a dominant gene in this family along with the blond hair. Joze quirked an eyebrow. "So you're the one always giving us trouble."

They all laughed. For once, it didn't come across forced.

Maddie started to pick up all the plates. Her nervous movements made it clear she was on edge. Was there anything he could do to assure her? He took another quick look at her mother. There was nothing she'd let him get away with even if her daughter was twenty-six and way past the age of being under a mother's thumb. Pushing down his frustration, Joze forced a fake smile.

Maddie's cousin rested her elbows on the table and leaned in. "I say we play board games. I need to get my mind on something else or I'm going to lose it. You, too, Joze. Unless you have work in the morning."

He rubbed the back of his neck and shrugged, working hard not to grin. Staying was exactly what he had in mind. "Aren't you all exhausted? I usually work second shift, so it's doable for me, but you've got to want to go to bed soon after being on the road."

He almost did a double take when Maddie didn't object or speak up against him staying. Was she coming around, recognizing the importance of his presence?

Games scattered across the living room floor, everyone but Mrs. Clare sat and argued over which one to play first. She'd disappeared once the games came out.

Maddie kept flitting her gaze to him. Was it a somewhat shy glint in her eye? For once her tough girl act wasn't overshadowing everything that passed between them. But he had to admit the tough girl was who she was. And he'd loved her once for it. Hmm. But he'd seen the vulnerable side of her in the past day too. What a surprise that she'd let him. That side of her was just as appealing.

Maddie moved some tendrils of hair out of her face, and his fingers itched. He remembered how it felt to stroke her silky hair. Joze struggled to get the thought out of his head.

But maybe he didn't need to.

19

Devin dropped the fake money into his hand. "I think we all need some snooze time."

Two in the morning. Wow. Joze pushed to his feet. He'd tried to keep the games going as long as he could, but when Aster's head actually landed on the game board, it was time to go. Even Maddie's eyelids drooped and looked like a kid coming off a caffeine high about ready to crash into the nearest soft object and pass out. And he'd been more focused on Maddie's sweet lips than taking his turn. More than once he'd had to play off the track of his thinking when Devin stared him down. Could they work things out? Was he ready to really forgive and take a chance with her? The gaming had brought their natural companionship out like it'd been when they were in college. And he liked it. Why keep denying his feelings for her?

Note to self, find Todd and drill him on that day four years ago.

Maddie rubbed her face. "Let me walk you to the door."

He followed her and tried not to look at the curvy shape of her body the whole way there. She tried to hide it some but...

He clamped down his thoughts. How did he ever think it possible to stay away from her when he was putting himself at her disposal every chance he got?

Maddie slowed as they drew closer to the door. She looked over her shoulder at him and gave a small smile. "Thanks for tonight. They needed a break from reality."

What about her? Was she OK that he'd stayed? Her quick glances and lingering fingers meant something, didn't they? "And you?"

They were out of sight of the living room where they'd been playing, but she peeked over as if she didn't want anyone to see them. He looked back. They were alone.

"Joze, I don't want you to get the wrong idea." Instead of pulling back as he'd expected, she put an unsteady hand on his chest.

Was she giving in to the truth of how good they were together? He willed his heart to stay steady but it trampled to a heavy beat. Please don't let her notice. He held his breath. He was losing the battle. With fingers as steady as he could muster, Joze put a firm hand on her elbow and willed the tingles to stay at bay. "What idea is there to get?"

She pulled him by his shirt a step closer. He couldn't stop the overwhelming desire her gesture and their closeness created. He leaned down, millimeters from her lips. "You make me crazy."

She closed her eyes. Her breath caressing his cheek, and she whispered, "Joze."

Now she'd done it. He couldn't hold back. He nuzzled her nose with his and closed his eyes.

A second later, Maddie shoved him back, and he jerked into alert mode. "What?"

Feet scuffed the wood flooring behind them. Good thing he caught his balance. Aster padded past them and up the stairs.

With a sigh, Maddie got on her tiptoes to see over his shoulder. "I'm coming."

Aster didn't turn but raised a hand.

What was he supposed to do now? She'd almost let him kiss her. No mistaking it.

Control. It was going to take a lot from here on out. He raked a hand through his hair and dared to move close to her again. Shouldn't he be fighting to stay apart? He didn't let the thought win.

Maddie bit her lower lip, her eyes not quite meeting his. "I've been taking all your time up. Sorry about that."

He put a hand on her shoulder and enjoyed the warmth that met his fingers. "I want to. Besides, I have a few days off this weekend."

She looked so unsure, almost scared. He wanted to stroke her cheek so badly, but he didn't.

When she settled her fingers on his forearm, he nearly went mad. This wasn't the same Maddie who'd pushed him away even yesterday. Was he ready to meet their past head on at all costs?

Devin cleared his throat at the living room door. "See you tomorrow, Joze?"

Maddie flinched, but this time he didn't remove his hand. An invitation.

Maddie piped up. "Oh no, he has things to do."

Huh? Hadn't she heard him? "What's on the docket for tomorrow?"

"I figured you'd be here for Maddie, that's all."

And he wanted to be. "Sure."

Devin rested against the door frame. "Hey, we could have a cook-off like the old days, cuz."

Another competition. Joze was game. "I'll bring

my famous Reuben sandwiches. The guys down at the squad will tell you they're the best."

Her cousin pumped the air. "You're on."

With arms folded, Maddie looked from one to the other. "You think the others will be up to it? I heard Jocelyn is having a very hard time right now—me too."

Devin's hands went up. "It'll keep us from perseverating." His voice had a catch in it on his next words. "And mom wouldn't want us to...wallow."

She gave in with lowered eyes. "True."

Devin wasn't going away. That meant Joze wasn't going to be acting on any of the pent-up emotions swirling his belly. He gave her shoulder one last squeeze. "Set the alarm."

She nodded. "Make it dinner time, OK?"

He fairly skipped down the steps on his way to his car. Joze rummaged through his pockets for his keys.

He breathed in the cool moist air of night, a slight breeze of pine floating toward him. Should he stay a while? There were plenty of people in the house for safety, and Maddie'd promised to sleep in Aster's room.

He peered into the black woods filled with the chirp of frogs and then down both directions of the street. All clear.

Hitting the unlock button, Joze reached for the door handle and opened it.

A flash of something...someone moving fast cleared the front of his car. He jerked back but not before something hard glanced off his forearm. Ow. "Who—"

The attacker raised his arm again. His raspy voice husked out like sandpaper against wood. "I said stay away from her." The object connected with the side of

Joze's head. "But you don't want to listen."

He crumbled to the ledge of the doorframe, one arm hooked between the car and the door itself. "Stop."

His world shifted and spun. Why couldn't he make his legs pull him up? The guy couldn't get away this time. Joze couldn't allow him to.

He managed to stand. Took a step. The asphalt under him wobbled. "Don't you—go near—her."

A streak of brown jacket vanished behind him. He ducked. Not another hit. It would finish him for sure. He tried to spin around but wobbled against the car. Fire seared his brain.

The perpetrator, hood covering his head, careened into the driver seat of a tan car parked in the neighbor's drive. He sped away.

With bleary eyes, Joze tried to make out the license plate. OMJ. Then was it an eight-six-nine? He repeated the letter-number combination over and over and collapsed into his car as carefully as he could. With his phone in hand, he put the numbers into his memo app. Every movement sent shockwaves of pain through his eye sockets. Should he go back to the house, call emergency services? His buddies could do a number on this guy now that he had something trackable.

If he landed on the Clare doorstep right now, there'd be too many questions, and Maddie was bent on keeping it from the family. He couldn't.

And he couldn't leave now either.

Joze reached up and touched his head. Something warm and wet coated his fingers. He winced.

He knew who to call. With one eye closed, he dialed David Beaucamp's cell. He worked the third shift for the police department, and they'd talked the other day about getting together for a game over the weekend. He was on patrol tonight. When his friend answered with a snide remark he held in his own response and got to the point. "Hey, can you do a license plate check for me?"

"How much is it worth to you?"

"Dude, I don't have time to mess around. I just got hit and now the guy's run off. OMJ8690."

His friend's voice chopped to attention. "Where are you? What do you mean you got hit? Your car or you?"

Joze pulled the phone away from his ear an inch. The tense voice of his friend exacerbated the drumming pain. "Me." He gave the address. "Don't come with blaring sirens and lights."

"What?"

"I'll explain when you get here."

"Sure, man. I'm on my way."

Joze parked his car in the Clare driveway. No way was he going to let the guy think he'd run away. And he wanted to be very visible. Joze grabbed some napkins out of the console and put them against his head with gentle pressure.

David pulled along the curb. He shined his spotlight on Joze, who waved at him with furious movements. "Turn that thing off."

David threw the switch and deadened the light. He stalked over to Joze, his slick black hair catching a glint of light from the streetlamp. "You tied up in that stalker case Tuttle has?" He looked to the house. "Is that why you're here?"

"Something like that." Small town, loud gossip. It hadn't gotten past the force, had it? He looked up to meet David's eyes. His buddy was a good six inches taller than him, but Joze didn't let it get under his skin that he was on the small side. "It's personal, really."

"I'm supposed to be on the other section of town. You should call Tuttle."

"You know why I can't do that." He wasn't ready to have Tuttle talking to Maddie again right now. Not with the family around. They walked over to the police cruiser. It was nice having friends in the force and on the squad.

"Let me guess, you want me to keep this under wraps?"

Joze nodded.

"Well, here's the info on that plate." David bent into his cruiser and looked at the computer screen attached to his dashboard. "Registered to a red pickup. I put a BOLO out for it."

"Whoa, stop there. This man was in a tan, four-door sedan, a Chevrolet. Late model."

"I need to call that in, then. Sounds like stolen plates."

Joze dug around in his mind. Wait, something wasn't right about the numbers. Were his eyes that blurry or were the numbers taped to make different ones? He had to think for a moment. "Um, I don't think so. More like he taped the numbers to appear different. They were a little uneven."

David had his mic in his hand. "OK. And..."

"Keep this quiet, OK? Think you can let me in on anything you find?"

"Yeah, of course. But you do know there could literally be thousands of vehicles in all the possible combinations, right?" He spoke the information into his mic, talking back and forth with the dispatcher on the other end. Then he turned back to Joze. "By now he could've removed the tape, but we'll do what we can."

"Figured as much." Joze pulled the napkins away from his head. The bleeding had stopped. There wasn't enough to need stitches. "Wanna get a picture of this for the report?"

His friend went to work on filing his statement and taking photos of the wound on his head and arm. "He got you good. You should have it checked out."

"I wish I'd gotten a punch in." How had he allowed the guy to sneak up on him? "But I think it's fine. I don't need to go in for this." A terrible guard he turned out to be. What had he been thinking about to distract him that much? He returned to the moments leading up to the attack. He had done a sweep of the area. But still. The sedan was parked on the far side of a neighbor's car. He should've noticed it.

Joze went back to his vehicle and looked at the spot from where the guy had sped off. He couldn't see the location where the sedan had been. He then moved to the sidewalk leading to the Clare house. He couldn't really see it from there either without craning his neck. No lights illuminated the area. And trees flanked both sides of the cement drive.

The perp had to have been waiting in the trees by his car. Plain and simple. What he wouldn't give to be able to cut all those trees down right now. Could he find a way to put spotlights on the wooded area?

David followed him. "I'll do a sweep of the area and get out of here."

So much for Joze heading anywhere but the front seat of his car.

20

Maddie raced to grab the phone off the receiver. "Can't anyone hear this thing ringing?" Into the phone, she said a breathy hello.

"This is Mrs. Canney from Anby Church. I am so sorry for your loss." When she spoke a moment later, her voice shook. "Lonna was a dear friend and prayer partner."

Maddie had to hold in her own shaky sob at the weeping of the woman on the other end. Had Aunt Lonna mentioned her before? She wasn't sure. There'd been lots of church friends she'd spent time with. "I'm calling to see if you wouldn't mind if some ladies from the church provide meals over the weekend. We want to make your load a little easier, what with the funeral and all on Sunday."

It took Maddie a second to speak. All morning, tears had threatened. It had started with Aster determined to go through some of Aunt Lonna's things, and now she couldn't shake the gloom that hovered. "That's so kind…thank you."

Oh wait, there was supposed to be the cooking thing with Joze and Devin tonight. But still, it would be nice to have extra food around. And it would make things easier to have meals already prepared for the next day.

"Could I bring a casserole around eleven?"

Maddie checked the clock on the stove: 9:30 AM. It would give them time to finish what they'd started in Aunt Lonna's room. She also needed to get back to reading the journal. "We'll be here. Thanks."

"If you need anything else, let me know, OK, honey?"

She wiped her face. The woman's grandmotherly tone comforted Maddie. It reminded her so much of Aunt Lonna.

She hung up before she had a full meltdown with the complete stranger, and ran up the stairs to her room. Pressing her back to the closed door, Maddie didn't bother to hold in her sobs. The whole month had been a complete nightmare. The plane crash, the journal, the stalker, all of it unreal. Yet she had to face it, had to figure it out. "Aunt Lonna, why'd it have to be your flight?" She cried. "What were you involved in?"

She fell into the computer chair at her desk. How was it possible to be so alone with a house full of people, and people who had more right than her to cry? She was only a niece. Yet she felt the pain of Aunt Lonna's loss so thoroughly she could barely catch her breath. She'd lost more than an aunt. As she'd told Aunt Lonna many times, she'd been her real mother. The one she could always talk to. The one who understood her. The one who hadn't abandoned her when her father died.

A soft knock at the door quieted Maddie. "Yes?"

Aster's muffled voice carried through. "You OK? I thought you were going to help me in Mom's room?"

She couldn't. Not now. But what could she say? "I...need a break, OK?"

"OK. I'll just be in there working on her desk."

Maddie looked to the heavens. "'K."

She pulled out a tissue and blew her nose. Maddie reeled from the full reality of loss with the force of a rock falling on her chest. She'd managed to keep it at bay the past week but now it crippled her with tears.

Where was God in all this? Maybe she didn't believe, but Aunt Lonna did. And if she was His child as her aunt claimed, wouldn't He take care of Aunt Lonna? This was proof that if He existed, He didn't care.

Anger replaced grief. It burrowed even deeper in her.

Be strong. Maddie tried to constrain the emotions welling through her body. *Stop it.* Fanning air into her face, she gulped in breaths. Control came in small waves. There was no changing what happened. What she could do was finish the investigation Aunt Lonna had started. It would be the final hurrah to her aunt.

Maddie ran to the bathroom and washed her face and freshened up the light amount of makeup she wore.

In her bedroom, she fished through the little cubbyhole built into the wall behind her bed for the journal, the musty odor of dust and old cloth emanating into her room.

She dusted some sticky webs off the book and set it on her desk. Aster needed to know she wouldn't be back for a while. She opened her door a hair and yelled down the hall, "Aster, I've got some things to do. Sorry. Can't help."

Her cousin grumbled but shut the door before she responded. The journal was more important.

After tucking a foot under her, Maddie found the last place Joze had read and fingered the page at the spot he'd stopped.

Each page resounded with more sadness. Her aunt had been so busy, helping with church activities, going on shopping dates with friends, the business, the reunion. Her head reeled. How could one person accomplish so much?

Several entries about the reunion showed a lot of contention. No one agreed on the venue or the price of tickets. The number of helpers dwindled over the course of months, putting a heavy load on Aunt Lonna.

Maddie set the book on the desk and yawned. She needed a cold glass of water. Her tongue rubbed against the inside of her mouth like cotton. She threw a few college papers over the book and headed downstairs. As she turned at the bottom step, she caught a few shadows falling over the front door side light.

The doorbell rang. Must be the lady with the casserole.

She turned off the alarm, plastered a smile on her face, and threw the door open.

A dark Hispanic man stood in front of her and then grabbed and pulled her. Her feet almost gave out under her as she tried to wrench out of his strong grasp. Her breath hitched in her throat, and she flailed her arms. To no avail.

"Madeline Clare?"

She gulped, eyes bouncing from one man to the other two over his shoulder. Lots of tattoos everywhere on the men's arms and even their necks. Matching shirts. Gangsters on her lawn? "Who are you?"

Belatedly, she noted the souped-up Dodge Challenger at the curb with flames painted along the back fender.

He yanked her up. "RoRo. You mess on my pad, I mess on yours."

Maddie pulled back her foot and kicked with all her might.

He managed to back away before she connected.

"Let go of me."

With his shove, she slid to the ground but he lowered his frame until his face was within a foot of hers. "Got your card from Beth."

Why'd she put her address on the thing? *Why, why, why?* How could she have made such a mistake to hand the card to the woman? Beth was supposed to call her when he showed up, not give him the card. She flipped between rage and fear so fast her head spun.

RoRo's thugs stepped closer still, cigarette smoke permeating off them. He folded his hands in front of him, displaying a distorted number seven tattoo on one forearm. "What do you want with me?" He reached out to her, a sneer mucking up his face. "You're not the usual kind I work with. But..."

She pushed against the hard clapboard siding of the house but didn't manage to gain more than a few inches away from him. Her voice shook and heat climbed up her neck. "I...I'm looking for information on my aunt. Your—name was in some of her paperwork and I need to know why."

His eyes bulged. "Your aunt, huh?"

Was he the stalker? She melted against the splintery floorboards of the porch. Where was Joze when she needed him?

"And who's your aunt?"

Please don't let any of the cousins come out now. Maddie looked from the closed door to RoRo, straining to remember every detail. A killer? "Lonna Selby."

He narrowed his gaze. The men behind him shuffled from one foot to the other, watching every passing vehicle and every movement in close proximity. He stood as fast as he'd dropped to a squat. "Let me tell you what. You do something for me and we'll talk?"

Maddie sprung to her feet, hands out, ready to deflect another move from him. False bravado could only get her so far, but she gave it everything she had. "I don't help drug dealers and trafficking junkies."

His face went dead cold. "Watch it."

She blinked and shrank back, fists flying into the air. As though that'd stop someone with his girth. "You've been stalking me?"

His two men laughed and pushed at each other. The shorter one teased, "Girl has guts."

RoRo jumped at her like a bulldog jerking on the end of its chain, and she jolted backward. He gave a hoarse laugh that sent him into a coughing spell. Reaching into his oily jeans pocket, RoRo pulled out an inhaler and then sucked a couple breathes from it.

Once he gained his composure, his narrowed gaze didn't make Maddie shudder as hard this time.

Now, his buddies were looking everywhere but at her as they scratched at their temples and pretended to ignore the asthmatic outburst.

He dropped his shoulders. "You'd know if I did. You change your mind, come back to Rusk Street."

Movement behind the men plummeted her stomach even more until the dark head of Joze came into view. She nearly passed out from relief.

Joze stormed up the stairs. "Sir, you need to back off now." His hand was at his side on something at his waist.

A gun? A paramedic who carried a weapon. She didn't have time to appreciate the irony. Maddie held her stance.

RoRo and his gang members stalked down the steps, pulling a cloud of soiled clothing and oil stench with them. "Dude, she's something."

Joze's tight form didn't flinch when they passed.

Unable to control the whirl of a tornado in her chest, she rushed to his side. Maddie clamped her jaw tight and held her stance until they climbed into their neon orange car with all the trimmings and drove off. Once they pulled into the street, screaming music fractured the neighborhood.

The next second, Joze turned, eyes flashing. His own voice ricocheted around the yard almost like the awful music had. "You see what happens when you go places you shouldn't?" His hands went to his head. "Next thing I know you'll be working for him."

Well that settled it. She couldn't tell him RoRo's proposal for sure, now. He'd never understand if she had to do something to get what she needed from the punk.

"Why would you ever open the door to a gangster? Didn't I warn you enough about him?"

"Well, at least he's not the stalker."

"How do you know for sure?"

She flinched. "He said so."

"So now you believe a thug?"

Maddie winced, her response coming out shaky, "Yeah."

He looked like he might kick something or punch the white column on the porch. "Maddie," he yelled, "When are you going to start listening? Men like him don't stop once they get a hold of you."

Who did he think he was? She stood her ground. "I don't need you to lord over me and tell me what to do. You get out of here." What'd happened to the thick relief of a moment ago? No one was going to yell at her like that again. "I mean it."

He balled his fists. "Fine. Get yourself killed—or worse," he sputtered as he passed her. "See ya."

Before she could reason out her response, he'd jumped in his car and peeled away. Great. Devin would be furious she'd ruined the cook-off.

She stormed up the steps. How dare—

"You must be Maddie. Well, Madeline."

She froze, heat wrapping around her neck and up to her cheeks. The declaration matched the voice of the woman who'd called earlier about the food. Had the woman heard the huge fight? She squeezed her eyes shut. "Yes?" It would take more than a second to gain her composure after that blow up.

"I'm here with the casserole." It came out more as a question.

Maddie spun around and waved her hand in the air. "Sorry about that."

Mrs. Canney's face stayed blank. "I know what pressure you're under."

An awkward silence fell between them. She put her hands out. What to say? "Can I take the dish?"

"It's my mac and cheese casserole." She handed over the thirteen by nine pan stacked with a few other containers. "And there're some green beans and a fruit salad there too."

They looked at each other. All Maddie wanted to do was disappear behind the door. "I—we appreciate your effort."

"I'll see you at the service." The woman scuttled

away before Maddie could come up with a reply.

Good grief. She'd offended one of Aunt Lonna's close friends.

21

Nothing could take Joze's mind off the blowout with Maddie. He stalked back and forth in his apartment, stepping over a pile of clothes to go in the wash. Now that RoRo was in the picture, the ante had been raised. Why couldn't Maddie listen to him? If she thought he'd stay away now, she had another thing coming to her. He'd keep an eye on her even if she didn't know about it.

He stopped. Why was he so bent on protecting her? Let her take care of herself. He dropped onto the leather couch and picked up the remote. Staring at the black screen, he fumed. Women.

The edge of his Bible poked out from under a towel. He eyed it then looked away but the Holy Spirit tugged on him. Fine. He pulled it out and set it on his lap. Leaning back, Joze stared at the ceiling. "Lord, she won't let me in. Why can't she see how dangerous this situation is?" He paused, frowning, then ran a hand over the stubble on his chin. The Bible flipped open in his grasp and he looked down at the page it fell to in Philippians. It took a moment for the verse to register as he read. What was this? God seemed to blatantly be telling him it wasn't his job to make her listen or change. True. *But...* But he couldn't argue with the Almighty. He read a few more verses. And the one she needed was not him but God.

He sighed and set the Bible down beside him. "Is it OK with You if I at least keep an eye out for her?"

His chest swelled with the answer. Put the emphasis in the right place. Remember that God was in control and quit trying to force her to do his bidding. Now that one was going to be the hard part. But he would try.

Joze grabbed a quick meal then phoned his buddy down at the police station. "David, I need to get some info on RoRo. He's stepped into my neighborhood and I don't like it. Could you do a little recon on his current situation with the Hartford department?"

"Man, you're lucky I've got friends down there. Don't you know how hard it is to get anything from another precinct?"

"I've always been able to count on you. Why do you think I'm your friend?" Joze bantered. "You have the friends in high places I need."

David laughed. "If it wasn't for the time you saved me from that chainsaw accident in my yard I don't know if I'd put up with you."

"Then you won't mind also letting me borrow your truck for a few hours, would you?"

"Oh, come on. Last time you left junk all over it."

"No, I didn't. That was from your brother. Don't pin that one on me."

David scoffed. "Whatever. You know where the keys are. But have it back by seven. I have a date tonight."

Joze whistled between his teeth. "Nice. It's about time."

They sent verbal shots back and forth at each other before hanging up. Joze called a couple other police friends and lined up a few extra surveillance drives past the Clare residence at the steep cost of an all-expense paid baseball party at his house next week.

One last call. He dialed Mrs. Mathers. This frequent flyer, as they called them in the medical field, was like a grandma to him. And he'd been making EMT stops at her place for the past two years. Her health issue? Loneliness. One of the main diagnoses for several of the senior citizens in the town who called on a regular basis. When she picked up, he said, "Hello gorgeous."

She gave her usual giggle.

Joze loved the old woman even at her most medically non-compliant moments. "Did you take your diabetic meds at ten?"

"Yeah, yeah. And I remembered to eat with that other pill that keeps making me sick."

He laughed. "Good. I'm on a special job right now, so I won't see you for a few days. Don't make my buddies have to show up. I'll give orders for a few extra IV drips if you do, you hear."

She snorted. "You're going to use my fear of needles against me, huh?"

"I do what I'm forced to do."

"Fine. But if you stopped by, it'd make my day."

He settled into the cushions. "Wish I could."

They hung up.

Joze went back to pacing. RoRo was a dangerous element in the mix of everything. His name popped up on Joze's radar over and over with his church ministry to the poor of Hartford. Nothing good ever came of knowing RoRo. His hands played a nervous beat against his pant leg. Maddie couldn't become a victim of the brute man. Joze couldn't let it happen. He'd better get back over to the Clares', even if he had to work at a distance.

Four hours and three bags of popcorn later, Joze squashed the last paper bag and dropped it into a plastic trash bag on the floorboard of his friend's old restored pickup. He held the small binoculars to his eyes and peered through the woods beside Maddie's house. Good thing not all the trees were in full blossom. It made it a bit easier to see through them to the far side in the blinding sun of the spring day.

All the accusations from Maddie against Todd, all the denials from his friend circled in his mind. What was the full truth? Maddie held rigid to her statements. It was in her eyes too. Something fearful which had never been there before. Who would hold so tight to something even at the expense of losing another person if it wasn't true? And she'd lost him.

He put a hand over his mouth. But what of Todd's side of the story? Joze took it apart piece by piece. It could be a lie. He had a tiny gap in his story. One that Joze couldn't smooth out of the picture no matter how small and insignificant it seemed at the time.

Betrayal lit at the corners of his mind. Todd may actually be guilty. He could have hurt Maddie. What was the truth? Years that they could've been together had been wasted if Todd had tried to harm her.

Picking up his phone, Joze found his friend's number in his contacts and his thumb hovered over it. Todd had to answer. He had to.

As the phone rang, he fiddled with the buttons on the door.

No answer. At the beep of the answering machine, Joze drew his mouth closer to his phone. "Todd, call me."

Why was it when he wanted answers the most, he

had to wait?

He dropped the phone onto the cream-colored pleather seat beside him. He'd wait...because now his future depended on it.

A car passed, and he returned to watching the street. One of the neighbors passed again. He'd seen them coming and going all afternoon.

He needed to stretch. As he climbed out, he patted his side. Gun. Concealed carry license all in good standing. He'd better get a look at the neighbor's drive where the perp had parked last night. But how could he get over there to check without being noticed? Across the street were more trees. He'd have to chance a violation ticket to get in there and walk down 'til he reached a safe location to check it.

Looking both ways, he crossed the street, glanced back and forged deeper into the woods. No trespassing signs didn't litter the trunks of the trees. That was good. There was less of a chance of getting the police called on him. Maybe it was the reason the perp felt safe parking there.

He moved at a clip until he could see. All clear. Joze took another look through the binoculars as far down the street as he could see and then turned them on Maddie's house.

Someone moved through the living room. It must be the other cousin he hadn't met yet. What was her name? Something close to his, he remembered that much.

Maddie stepped into the light of the window in the library on the front right side of the house. He jerked back. She didn't see him, did she? He'd better get back to his car. She stepped out of sight, and he took off through the trees. His foot caught on something and he pitched forward. Good thing he had the binoculars on a strap tied around his neck. He'd never find them in the dead leaves from last fall that clogged the ground and killed any chance of fresh grass growth.

He got his feet back under him and made a beeline for the curb, out of view of the front door. With a hasty look back, he didn't see anyone exit the house. No one came around the side of the house from the back door.

It took him a second to get his breath. He climbed into his truck and scrunched down in his seat. Maybe he should circle the neighborhood and come back in a few minutes. But that meant he'd have his eyes off the property for too long. At least pull forward out of view a little more?

He moved the car twenty feet further away. Now he could only see the front yard. No view of the side; that wasn't going to work.

He could army crawl into the woods and hunker down on the ground.

Through his rear view mirror, he took another look back. Still dead calm reigned. He relaxed his shoulders and slowly sat up.

22

Maddie's heart kicked into third gear. She jumped back from the window and rounded the doorway. In the living room, she took another look through the windows as far as she could see up the street. A truck just out of full view sat on the side of the road. Wasn't it a little closer the last time she looked? She didn't recognize it. *Not again.* And in a truck this time, not the tan car? It had gotten so out of hand she was afraid to even go on her own front porch.

Anger welled all the way to her fingertips. Followed by a huge dose of fear.

What could she do? She couldn't live like this anymore. She had to show him he couldn't control her.

If the plan was to kill her, wouldn't he have done it by now? Was his tactic just to scare her into silence for something she didn't even know about? If the fear clogging her nerve endings would stop she'd go out and yell it on the top of her lungs that she didn't know anything. Didn't know why he was after her. But would it do any good?

She pulled back. She'd been through worse and she couldn't let this continue. She couldn't be a victim again.

She moved her hand to her pant pocket. The little pocket knife that never left her since she'd scouted it out of Devin's drawer wouldn't do any good unless she didn't mind getting up close and personal. And she did mind. Then what could she use? Devin had a bat somewhere. Please let it be in his room and not out in the garage. Maddie stopped. How was she going to explain to him why she wanted it?

She peeked into the kitchen. He slumped over a bar stool reading something. This wasn't the time to raise suspicion. She'd have to get it as fast as she could and leave his room before being seen.

Skipping steps, Maddie got to the top landing and checked for Jocelyn and Aster. The hall was empty. Music seeped out of Aster's room. She walked past her door as calm as she could and made sure her cousin wasn't paying any attention to her movement. Aster sprawled across the pink bedding from her youth, her head turned away. Maddie hurried into Devin's room. She checked his usual spot behind the door. It wasn't there.

She shook the frustration out of her body. Quick, check under the bed. Maddie lifted the comforter. The metal dinged-up bat caught the light. Yes.

She hurried to the door and put her back against the wall, checked the hall and scampered back down the steps, careful to hold it tight against her left side as she passed Aster's door.

Sliding her boots on, Maddie put her hand on the door and turned the knob. She froze. Disarm first. She scolded herself, reached for the buttons, and then put in the code.

One last look down the hall, and she stepped out the door and hunched down as close to the house as she could get.

The purple-hued truck gleamed in the sun. She grasped the bat in a tight grip. How could she get to it without being seen? She could take a full run at it. No. He'd have time to get out and grab her.

If she went around the garage she could go through the woods. She gave another look back to the kitchen. Devin mumbled out a few words to some song he must be listening to on his iPod. There would be no getting past him with the heavy bat unless she covered it. She'd have to scurry around and dash through the bushes to the back, too.

Maddie wrapped it in a blanket and made a run for the bushes, squatted down, and eyed the area. Once a car passed, she rushed to the garage and skirted the back of it. With eyes wide open, she took in the neighbor's backyard. Still nothing.

Into the woods, her skin prickled, her fingers tensed even tighter around the weapon in her hands. She stooped behind a few rock outcroppings on her way forward and dropped the blanket.

Now she'd have to crawl or risk being noticed. The person in the driver's seat remained hidden behind the tinted windows covering him.

She got on her stomach and crawled, slow and jerky.

Had she seen movement? Maddie didn't have a choice. She hurdled off the ground, and vaulted to the back of the vehicle. She raised the bat and slammed it against the back light, a scream belting out of her. "Why won't you leave me alone?" Her chest almost exploded from the racing of her heart. "I—don't— know—"

"What are you doing?" The driver thrust the door open and flew out.

Maddie slowed the bat as it descended upon the side of the truck a second time, but from the force of momentum, she couldn't stop it from bumping the two-toned paint job again. "Joze?"

Her legs jellied, and she grasped the side of the vehicle to keep from falling backward.

"What are you doing?" he yelled. His hands waved in crazy movements. "I can't believe you did that."

She couldn't look at him. Confusion clogged her to her pores. Why was he in this truck? The one that'd been parked for hours. How had she managed to screw this up and think it was the stalker?

His full force yelling ceased as he stopped and sucked in all the air around her. "My friend is going to kill me."

The bat clunked against the asphalt at her feet. She pulled herself up and braced against the truck, her hand going to her pounding head. "I...I didn't know...it was you. I thought..."

He was at her side before she could draw more oxygen into her lungs. "You try to stop me at every turn."

Nothing made sense. "But I told you to go. I didn't know it was you. I swear."

He shook a fist in the air. "You are more trouble..."

Now he'd said it. She pushed away from him and narrowed her eyes. "Listen, I didn't know it was you. I thought that creepy stalker was back, and I'm done with this whole thing. I want my life back."

He stopped ranting.

The heat of his body radiated against her skin. Why'd he have to be the most aggravating human being she knew?

His nose flared as he stared her down. She looked

away. The taillight. On an antique truck. Oh great. Where was she going to get the money to replace it? And how was she or he going to explain to the owner what happened?

In one fluid movement, Joze yanked her around the side of the truck.

He shoved her to the ground. Maddie tried to push out of his grasp, but he whispered into her ear, his hot breath tickling her to her core. "Stay down. It's the tan sedan."

She breathed in his sweet sweat and cologne, and tensed.

Two minutes too late. The bat could've done a number on the right car if she'd just waited.

She peered under the truck as the car passed in slow motion, and whispered, "Are you sure it's the right one?"

He pressed closer. "Shh. The license plate is obscured. Has to be."

Her side ached from the cold metal of the truck running board cutting into it.

Time seemed to slow so much she had to fight the urge to pull away from Joze's grasp and see for herself if the car was long gone. His proximity reminded her how much he had been there when she needed someone to lean on the most. He'd cared even when he didn't have to. She couldn't discount him anymore. What if...

Maddie flinched and tried to pull away mentally.

At that moment, Joze began to stand. "He's gone. Man, he's relentless. Thank God he didn't see us."

She refocused back to the road. And then tears threatened. What had she been thinking? She'd almost put herself straight into the stalker's path.

Joze pulled her to her feet. "Call Sam Tuttle. He has to know the guy's still around."

Had she crushed her phone against the road when they'd hidden? She got up and pulled it out. Oh, please let it be OK. There was no money to replace it if it was broken. Not after the tail light.

Its screen had a tiny crack in the bottom corner. She sucked in the flower-scented air in relief and dialed.

Joze threw open the door and pushed her up into the truck. "We need to be out of sight if he makes another round."

She nodded.

The officer took her information once the dispatcher connected her to him. "Ma'am, he's gone?"

"Yes."

"And you said you're with Joze Evans?"

"Yes, sir."

"I'll be there to patrol the area as soon as I can. It's been a busy day." He hung up.

How long could that take? She dropped the phone into her lap and relayed the information.

Joze propped a hand on the wheel, his gaze bouncing up and down the street. "We need to get out of here."

23

The flowers. The oppressive soft music in the background. All the people filling every corner of the house made Maddie want to vomit. How she'd managed to hold her back ramrod straight through the funeral service and keep back the tears was a true miracle. And now the cloying air of casseroles and salads made it just as hard to breathe. She swiped a fuzzy off her black, fitted dress and avoided yet another friend of Aunt Lonna's for the third time. Where had Joze gone? She couldn't shake him off her side since the truck incident yesterday until now.

If she could get outside to the air of freshly fallen rain, she'd be able to think. Sidestepping a group of talking guests, Maddie kept her head down. Don't look into any eyes. It'll stop people from trying to talk.

She rested against the outside back door, a cool breeze stirring her long hair. Devin and some old friends from high school passed a faded football back and forth. How lucky they were to forget the debilitating pain of Aunt Lonna's loss for a while. Why couldn't she?

Aster and Jocelyn sat under the tiny roof of the porch to Aunt Lonna's office outbuilding. The younger of the two wiped her face with a tissue. Obvious mascara marks streaked her face. Maddie wanted to bound over and comfort her as she had over the years, to play mother one more time to them both, but she held her ground. She didn't have anything to give them right now. And what would come out would be more damaging than good.

Aster caught Maddie's gaze. Maddie stepped back into the kitchen, pretending she didn't see them wave her over. They'd have to do this on their own. With her hand to her temple, she wished away the headache she couldn't completely shake since she'd hit her head. Good excuse to disappear into her room.

Someone touched her elbow. "Maddie?"

She blew out her cheeks and stopped. "Yes?"

Mrs. Canney stood beside her. An apology started to roll off her tongue.

The apricot-haired woman seemed to sense her need to have space. She backed up some. "I understand."

Maddie looked to the counters covered in food dishes. "I'm so thankful to you and your church for setting up all this food. I couldn't have pulled it together on my own." And Mom sure wouldn't have done it, either. But Mom could pay for it. "Can I give you a donation from our family?"

The woman's warm hand touched her arm. A look Maddie couldn't quite read passed over the woman's soft, wrinkled face. "No donation will get you to God."

She drew back, but the small hand remained and Mrs. Canney's face softened. "You should stop by some time to our lady's group. We meet every Monday night at seven."

Three days ago, she'd have been incensed by the remark. Now it just made her sad. That's where Aunt Lonna would've been if she were still alive. "I have to get back to college soon."

The woman dropped her hand. "Almost graduated, aren't you? Lonna was so proud you went back and finished."

Maddie startled. Did the woman know what had caused her to leave the first time?

A tiny smile fell across Mrs. Canney's lips. Kindness, not sympathy. "I'll stick around and clean up later. No worries."

With her hand to her heart, Maddie melted. She mouthed a thank you and headed for the stairs.

Joze moved into her path. She couldn't resist the touch of his hand. She grasped him back, the smooth material of his well-fitted black suit rubbing her palm. If she could only let herself fall into his embrace for a moment. Just one moment. It might all be better.

He seemed to sense her need. Pulling her into the bathroom, he closed the door and brought her close. She didn't resist. "You know you can cry. I haven't seen a tear all day."

No, she couldn't. Not with so many people watching. And they only had a moment before someone would be knocking to use the facilities. But oh, how good his arms felt around her. The suit turned him from super-hero-ambulance-junky to pure, rich civility. She stroked his arm as he held her. What she wouldn't give to turn back the days. Maddie tightened in his arms at the thought. Really? Maybe?

He breathed words into her hair. "Let God take this burden from you, Maddie."

Her back tightened, but she didn't completely pull away. "You and these church people. You know, Mrs. Canney was just harassing me with God. Why can't you let up and allow me to believe what I want?"

He didn't speak right away. She waited for a holy

roller diatribe. Instead, he pulled her closer. "Because I...care for you. I want you to have what I have. It's the only way to deal with all the awful things that have happened to you."

Was it an admittance that he believed her about the past, or was he referring to the last few days? "And?"

"And what? That's all." He nuzzled her neck.

She fought the tingles, the warmth of him, everything that made her want to let go and trust him. "And I have to have an apology from you."

He stopped. "For what?"

She pulled back to look in his eyes. "You know."

At that Joze released her and put his hands on his hips. "Can't you stop for one day?"

Great. Now the fighting would commence. Again. She swiped her hair away and yanked the door open with all her might, her lips in a taut line.

He didn't stop her. Maddie's heels clicked hard against the wood floor. When she reached the bottom step, the doorbell rang. The last thing she needed was another guest to try and comfort her. She slung the door open and ushered in a middle-aged gentleman. Must be another reunion friend. A couple ladies followed him in, pausing their talk long enough for him to give his condolences. Should she drill him about the reunion? She couldn't find the strength to do it today.

He moved to the living room where the majority of reunion friends were gathered. She sat on the third step. This would be the time to ask questions. Maddie glared at the group from between the stair spindles. Exhaustion and headache etched into her brain.

The bell rang again. Maddie squeezed her eyes

closed. How many more friends did Aunt Lonna have?

She stopped. Wait. One of these people could be the one following her. Was a tan car sitting along the street among the hordes of mourners' vehicles? She hesitated and then checked the hall and living room doorway. There wasn't one person looking in her direction or watching her movements.

With slow steps she moved to the door and pulled it open a little. Two more men in dark suits waited to be admitted, one behind the other.

They introduced themselves.

Maddie tried to hold onto at least their last names, but the headache made the task impossible. "Please come in."

They entered and dispersed into the crowd.

Once again, Joze had disappeared.

If she didn't get some medicine, she was headed for a full-out migraine. Maybe there was some ibuprofen in the bathroom. She edged the wall into the bathroom, closed the door, and reached in the mirrored cabinet for ibuprofen. She poured two into her hand, and then with a gulp of water from the sink she let them slide down her throat.

The clock ticked four. How much longer would she have to paste a smile on her face and talk?

A knock at the door made her groan. She pushed off the sink and strode out of the bathroom. Joze stopped her. "Did you hide the journal? There're too many unknowns here."

She stopped. Huh? Oh, true. "I did."

The crowd seemed to push in and her world tilted.

Joze's hands caught hers. He led her to her mom's room. "You better lie down." He peppered her with medical questions. Some of them were so personal that she almost reached out and slapped him. Once again, he felt her head but the headache got so bad she let him do his work and answered with minimal words. "Migraine. That's all."

He hovered. "Want me to talk to anyone specific?"

She sighed. "That would be great. I was wondering how I could pull it off. The group talking in the living room are the reunion coordinators." Her words began to slur. "See if they noticed anything unusual about my aunt right at the end. And find out if they know who K is."

"OK. I'm locking the door behind me."

Good idea.

"I'll be back in an hour. Just rest. Please."

She buried her head under a pillow to block out the light. It was only the second migraine she ever remembered having. Good thing, too, because it was excruciating.

24

A knock at the door pulled Maddie out of a light sleep and into flight mode. Her hand went to her temple. Where was she? She sat up on an elbow and remembered the migraine. And Joze.

Quiet reigned through the house. How long had she slept?

She slid over the side of the bed and padded to the door. "Joze?"

"It's me." With a shaky movement, Maddie opened the door. "Hey."

"Feeling any better?"

She rested her head against the doorframe. No shooting pain accompanied her movements. Good. "Yes. Just a little foggy, that's all."

"Everyone's gone." He pushed the door open a bit more, and she followed him out. "And they left lots of food."

What a relief. No cooking for a few days. Then she'd be back at college. All this would be behind her. She hoped.

She kept her eyes half-closed until she reached the kitchen where Mom and Jocelyn washed dishes.

Maddie ushered Joze to the hall. "Thanks for taking care of me."

"I hear a 'but' in that."

With her hand on the wall to steady her, Maddie

shrugged. "Can I have some private time with my family?" She rushed on when she saw the hurt in his eyes. "I'll call you later. I promise."

Joze waved her off. "It's fine. I do understand. But please call me."

She stopped on the porch. "Did you find anything out earlier?"

He leaped down the steps, swinging his suit jacket over his shoulder. He looked so good at the moment. The perfect gentleman. She reined in her thoughts and tried to pay attention to his words.

"One woman ticked off seven different men who went to school with her and Lonna and whose first names start with a K. Said there were probably more but she'd have to consult her lists. And they all seemed to be on a roll about getting as many people to attend as possible. Seems they have everything else lined up and in order. Someone asked your mother about some charts or something and she said she'd have to find them. But it didn't sound like a big deal. They all looked pretty genuine. Like good friends not hiding any big secrets."

The reunion didn't seem to be playing into the whole situation in any way. "Maybe we can scratch them off the list of suspects then."

He didn't turn. "Go back in the house and set the alarm."

"Bossy." She folded her arms across her stomach. "But OK."

Maddie closed her door. The blissful darkness of the room engulfed her. As her head hit the pillow, something was off kilter. She jumped up. Had someone been in there?

The desk chair lay at a different angle than she

remembered leaving it. She swung around. A shirt sleeve hung out of a dresser drawer. She never left them like that. She wanted to scream. Someone had been searching her room. But which one of the guests? Curses to the migraine that'd sidelined her so fast.

She scurried to the headboard of her bed. Her mattress didn't quite lay even on the box spring. Fisting her hands around her hair, she pulled it. "No, no, no!"

The journal was gone.

Tears stung so hard she had to let them fall. Her sobs brought Aster and Jocelyn running to her room. It hurt even more that she couldn't share the devastation with the closest people she loved. They tried to comfort her, and she didn't stop them. Even Devin popped his head in the door and waited for a command from her. She'd pass it off as grief for her beloved aunt. That's all they needed to know. And they needed to get back to their lives where they were safe again. She lifted her head. "When do you all leave?"

Aster laid her head on Maddie's knee. "I have a night class tomorrow. I was going to skip this week, but I think I need to get back, you know?"

Jocelyn sat back on her haunches. "Me, too. The semester ends in a month. I really can't miss."

Turning, Maddie caught Devin's eye. He looked away. "I have the week free."

Think quick. "We should let this all sink in, get together in a few weeks." Would it be enough time to lose the stalker? "I don't want any of you to fret over the house. I'll stay and do what absolutely has to be done for the rest of this week, but you need to get back to your lives."

They all fell silent.

She stroked Aster's hair. "OK?"

Everyone wiped their eyes and agreed. Relief rippled through her. The sooner they left, the safer they were.

Once everyone turned in for an early night, Maddie lay in her bed. What could she do? Joze needed a break. He had to be due back at work on Monday. She couldn't wake him now. But she had to do something. All chances of finding the answers in the journal were gone. For good.

And that left RoRo. Joze wouldn't even consider turning to the gangster. Which meant she was on her own.

25

Maddie had to leave...and now. She tapped her fingers and shifted from foot to foot. As much as she wanted to say good-byes to the cousins, this was taking forever. Aster gave her another hug, and Jocelyn joined in. "I love you two. I'm proud of you."

Jocelyn let go. "You sound like Mom. Knock it off."

"Really? I've always babied you two."

Aster kissed her cheek. "True."

Mom strode toward them in her usual frenzy of getting ready for work. "I'm going to miss you girls."

They wrapped their arms around her as they had Maddie. "We'll miss you too, Aunt Sassie."

Aster waved her fingers at Mom. "See you at graduation. Don't forget. And don't double book your schedule so you can't make it."

"I promise." Mom reached for one more squish from them.

Maddie pursed her lips. Why couldn't she get the same love and concern from Mom? And Mom wondered why Aunt Lonna was the one Maddie always turned to. Here was the proof, plain and simple.

She pressed her hand to her mouth and blew them a kiss. "Be safe."

Devin followed the others out the door. His quick

wave and nod made Maddie smile. After all these years he skipped hugs still. Old habits were hard to break.

Mom closed the door behind them and ran back to her room. "Hey, I have this deal over in Darien and it's not going well. I think I'm going to end up renegotiating the terms on the sale, so I'm staying there a few days to make things easier."

Maddie pursued her. "OK." She exhaled and wiped her brow. Now she didn't have to worry about Mom being safe. "Well, I'll be around if you need anything."

Mom dropped her mascara on the granite counter in her bathroom and peered at Maddie through the mirror. "Aren't you going back to college in a day or so?"

"By the end of the week. But I need to work on…a project. No disruptions." How much should she say to Mom? Things were way beyond dangerous. And it was about to get worse once she talked to RoRo.

Her mother threw some items into her attaché case and then studied her. "Is this about the other night? I thought all that was dealt with." She stopped her hyper movements and drew close to Maddie.

Oh, right. Mom didn't know everything that had happened. It was the price of trying to keep secrets—being alone in them. "Well…" Maddie scratched her head and then waved her hand. "Everything's under control. Don't worry about it."

"If you're sure." Mom took one more look at Maddie and then zipped the case.

With as much of a smile as she could muster, Maddie leaned against the bed. "Want help packing?"

"I already packed. But thanks for asking." Mom

wheeled out her designer suitcase from the closet and pulled a garment bag off the closet door. "I'll be home Wednesday."

"Bye."

Mom blew her a kiss and marched out the door.

Maddie's hands shook. She got in her car. How irrational could she be to do this thing with RoRo? The stress and constant high-strung awareness was getting to her, and now she was being dangerous. Maddie set Joze's number in her phone to call him with the push of a button if something went awry.

She stuffed the phone in her pocket and pulled out of the drive. Thick, rolling clouds hung low, sending a cold wave of temperature through Connecticut.

26

Joze's phone sang at his side, only the menacing ringtone of Freddie Cougar he'd originally set to Maddie's number made his heart flip with something akin to joy instead of the terror it was meant to bring. He set the sterilization wipes down on the stretcher he'd been cleaning and answered. "Hello?"

Muffled sounds filtered through as if material or something was rubbing against the cell. "Hello? Maddie?"

She was talking. "I can't believe I'm doing this."

He felt his skin crawl. "Maddie, Maddie. What are you doing?"

She seemed to be talking to herself and didn't answer him. Had she butt-dialed him? "RoRo better be there."

A butt-dial for sure.

He put his hand over his phone and yelled to Jim. "I have to go. Stretcher is clean."

He didn't give them a chance to respond as he bolted to his car and burned rubber out of the parking lot.

Why was she looking for RoRo? His blue tooth in the car brought the soft sound of her radio through the speakers. That meant she was going to the one place he'd told her never to go alone. His pulse beat at his temples and shot pounding blood through his ears.

That woman.

His grip on the steering wheel was sure to leave permanent marks. He hung up and waited an interminable five seconds to call her back. When she picked up on the third ring, he didn't wait for niceties. "Where are you?"

She sputtered but no words came out.

"You accidentally called me. I know where you're headed, and you can't do it."

She groaned.

A light flicked red in front of him. He braked but not fast enough to stop from blowing through it. Good thing the coast was clear. "I know how desperate you must feel, but he's only going to make things worse." He softened his voice. "Can we meet at the diner? You know the one we ate at last time?"

It took her a second to answer. "OK."

He covered his mouth with his hand. What should he say to her? If he yelled and ranted the way he wanted, she'd write him off for good. So what could he do?

Joze began praying and didn't stop until he pulled into the restaurant parking lot.

He held the door open and ushered her in. Maddie glanced back at him several times, fear etched in every muscle move. "I'm sorry, Joze. I just want this to be over."

They took the same seats in the back, and he drew in a few cleansing breaths. "I know you do but not like this."

She played with her nails and bit her lip. "Someone stole the journal last night."

His calm dissolved, but he fought to keep an even voice. "I had my eye on everyone. I never saw anyone go into your room."

She picked at a hangnail, trying to peel it free. "Except when we were in the bathroom."

Right. He closed his eyes. Those sweet moments where she'd let him hold her. Where he'd have given almost anything to have her with him forever. Why hadn't he insisted on keeping the journal with him where it would've been safer? "How did that lead you back to RoRo?"

She licked her lips. "He told me last time if I did something for him, he'd give me what I wanted." It didn't surprise Joze that she refused to look at him. "I had no choice. Without the journal, there's no way to figure out who's after me. He was the only other lead."

"I see." He reached for her hand to still its constant movements. She clenched his hands, and he widened his eyes. He'd expected her to pull away and now her supple hands yielded in his. It made him want more. But what a time to be thinking of such things. "There has to be another way." Oh, how he wanted to say so much more than that but the amount of control he'd garnered so far astounded him.

Maddie avoided his gaze.

God, I know You're testing me here and I'm about to fail. Help. "You do understand that he won't let you go once he gives you any info, right? That's what I'm trying to get at. In his eyes, you'll always owe him."

Her body jittered as her knee bounced up and down. "There's always a first time for everyone."

He could pull up a story or two on the gangster that would curl her straight hair. "You need to stay away from him. I mean it. For your own good."

The waitress sauntered over and took their order. Maddie looked like a death row inmate who got a stay of execution notice.

He swung his regard to the waitress and ordered his usual, all the time smelling the onions and peppers floating his way on a cloud of steam from a nearby serving tray and then waited for her to walk away.

Weariness poured off her. "But I'm no closer to figuring out what happened. I need a break in this thing. And I don't know where else to turn."

"How in the world did your aunt hook up with RoRo? He's not from Anby or anything?" He ran an arm along the back of the booth and rested it along the top. And she didn't seem like the drug type when he'd met her years ago.

She dropped her head onto her folded arms on the table. "I don't know. And without the journal, I don't think we'll ever figure it out."

We? Was he getting somewhere with her?

He worked to make a connection. "Could the illusive K. in the journal be a doctor at one of the offices? Do you think that's why she had the address to the building we checked out? Someone that important could be very dangerous to cross."

"Maybe?" Her voice crept up a little higher.

"K. was her boyfriend. It would be devastating to realize someone you loved is involved in crime. It would also explain why she seemed upset."

Maddie played with her straw, swishing it around in her drink. "You think he discovered she was investigating him?"

"Has to be." He shook his head. "But I don't get why he'd go after you."

She stopped stirring her straw. "She told me everything. Even things she wouldn't share with Mom. But her life was boring. There wasn't much to tell."

Maddie eyed him. "He must've known that somehow. But she kept all this to herself for once."

"Yeah, the one time she should've told you—or someone." Joze unfolded and refolded his napkin. "There could be evidence against him at your house."

"I think it's time to go back to Aunt Lonna's office. There has to be something up there." She dropped her chin. "Well, if the stalker didn't find it when he was up there originally."

Joze reached over and rubbed her arm, his calm returning bit by bit as if he'd put the pin back in a live grenade. "What about your family?"

She sighed. "They all left this morning. Mom even headed out on a business trip for a few days."

Maddie had always put her family first, protecting them like a fierce mama bear. What would it be like to be in that inner circle of hers again? Did he want that?

He studied her. Before he could even think about whether or not to let her back in his world, he needed to catch the man who was out to get her. But it was getting harder and harder to keep his distance and his thoughts about her at bay. Even the touch of her hand sent his senses into overdrive. If only the dreaded day four years ago had never happened.

27

Maddie unlocked the back door and scurried into her kitchen, the cold fingers of the empty house reaching out and bringing her to full attention. Whatever happened to the warmth of spring days? She reset the alarm and then ushered Joze past her, where the bright sun dropped patches of a kaleidoscope pattern on the tiled floor and counters. For once, the headache from her fall had subsided on its own. She must be getting over it. Finally. Now, time to tear the house apart. The stalker needed to be behind bars, and they had to find something to put him there.

She put her keys in her pocket and dropped her purse beside the coffee machine. "Out to the office?"

Joze rested his hands in his pockets. "If you think it's the best place to look. What about her room?"

"We're going to search every inch of this house." Maddie took the key to the office off the cat-shaped key holder and rearmed the alarm. Then they went out.

On the top step of the office, Maddie paused and took in the mess. How were they ever going to be able to decipher what had significance and what didn't? She scratched her head and looked from one end of the large room to the other. "Should we work together, or each take a different end?"

Joze quirked his mouth. "We can get more done if we work separate but..."

She read into his uncertain stance. "I know. That's what I'm thinking. Well, I'll start at her desk. You can start over there." She pointed to the large table in the far corner of the room. "Mind picking up those filing cabinets?"

Joze stalked over and lifted the first one to right it.

She moved to the desk and fought the urge to lovingly run her fingers along the edge of the desk that Aunt Lonna had restored years ago. Maddie climbed under the table and began piling papers on top of each other. When the floor was clear around the desk, she went from her knees to the desk chair, carrying the papers with her. With the stack on the table, she worked through them one by one. Most were invoice orders Aunt Lonna had printed from her online business. Soap supply orders and a few receipts for party supplies were mixed together. She separated them. Perhaps the reunion committee wanted everything pertaining to it. "Hey, set anything that looks like it has to do with the reunion to the side."

"OK."

She pulled out one slip and read it. "Aunt Lonna ordered three hundred balloons, some fake columns, even doilies for the tables. Sounds like it was going to be a nice party."

"Uh-huh. There's one over here for seating arrangements."

Maddie set her paper down and went to his side. "I wonder if that's the paper Mom had said one of the members was looking for."

He handed it to her, his fingers grazing hers. How good it was to have someone in all this mess—Even Joze—especially Joze. He put her first. Again. Who else would do that as much as he had in the past days?

She looked at his bent head and the desire to run her hands through his hair was almost irresistible. Her hand hovered just over the nape of his neck. *Don't do it.* In a soft voice, she murmured, "Thanks Joze. You've been here for me through so much."

He turned, smiled, and then gazed at her, a question in his eyes.

Yes, she'd admitted it. She needed him, indeed wanted him for more than physical protection. But how could she let herself say it out loud? Was this a moment of weakness, or did she really care about him? Love him? "Um…"

Maddie pulled away, slow and unsure, and planted her feet. "We better get back to work."

He got up and stepped close to her. "What if I don't want to?"

She studied the ground, the past hanging between them. "Look, Joze." She paused. What could be said? It'd all been rehashed over and over and they'd been at a stalemate before.

28

The crowing of the rooster ringtone on his phone startled Joze. Todd's ringtone. Adrenaline raced through him as he glanced at Maddie and took in her crossed arms and questioning look. This was the worst time—no, the best time—to talk and clear the air regarding four years ago. He held up a finger for Maddie to give him a minute and then slid the talk button to the right as he raced down the stairs and out the door.

How many times had he tried to reach Todd over the past couple days? He clenched and unclenched his left hand as he tried to formulate words in his mind. "Hey." What would it take for Todd to tell him the truth? A call on the old brother code they'd used as kids? Todd wouldn't dare renege on that.

Todd's jovial voice held its usual laughter. "Long time no call, buddy."

Joze's tone went cold. "Why didn't you return my calls?"

"Whoa. I've been on vacation, OK?"

Joze's heart rate skyrocketed into overtime. Should he go hard and fast or start out easy? No, hard and fast. *Please don't lie to me.* "Tell me what you did to Maddie Clare. Now."

Todd sputtered, "You know."

"Don't lie to me," he bit out. "I've heard her side,

and I know you tried something with her. But I want to hear the truth from you." He could forgive, but he'd never have another thing to do with Todd again once the words were out. The ones he knew in his heart to be true.

"Fine." He went into his side of the story, this time admitting it had been an attack, yet trying to explain how it was Maddie's fault.

Joze swallowed the bile in his throat. All these years he'd trusted Todd. Looked out for him as a brother. And shielded him. Now the truth lay before him like a scene played out in his nightmares. "Good-bye."

Todd tried to stop him from hanging up. "We've been friends since we were in diapers. You can't do this, Joze. Not over her."

Anger shot black spots into his eyes. Joze didn't answer.

"I...I..." When Todd stuttered, Joze pulled the phone away from his ear and began to hang up, but then put it back. "It was a mistake. But I can't take it back now."

"A mistake?" he yelled. "I can't believe you—It's going to take a lot more than that for you to fix this. Don't be surprised to find charges pressed against you."

"Whoa, stop there. She can't."

"She can. And I'll make sure she does." He wished it were possible to punch Todd through the phone. "I can't deal with you right now—maybe never again." The fact that he'd believed his friend over Maddie cut deep into his heart.

Joze looked up to the window of the office. How was he going to fix this? How could he take back all the pain and agony he'd caused her and expect forgiveness? Once he told her about the call, she'd explode. And there would be no coming back. No amount of groveling was good enough to make up for his lack of trust. But the days had been building up to this precipice. Joze had to make it right, even if it meant losing her again.

He hit the end call button and dropped his hand to his side, squeezing his eyes shut. What to say? How to say it?

Please God, see me through this.

Joze slowly made his way back up the to the office. Each step affirmed that he was certainly going to lose Maddie again.

29

Maddie glimpsed a shadow on the floor moving in her direction. She flinched and spun around, but only Joze stood at the top of the stairs. He rubbed the back of his neck and clenched his jaw. Alarm raced through her. What had elicited the pained look in his eyes? "Something happen?"

With heavy, slow steps, he reached for her and pulled her into his arms. She blinked. "What?"

Shuttering his eyes, he pressed his forehead to hers, taking a breath. When he opened them again, his grip tightened around her and she dared not move. Bad news for sure.

"Please, start talking before I lose it. What happened? Are you OK?"

He looked to the ceiling. A prayer sent heavenward?

Maddie took in every fiber of his being that touched her. How she wanted to stay secure in his arms. Yet she couldn't.

He pulled away an inch and rested his hands on her upper arms. "That was Todd on the phone."

Ice ran through her veins, creating a shiver. Maddie dropped her hands and went stiff as she trained her gaze on his. Had he admitted the truth? She tried to read Joze's expression.

"He admitted to it. And…"

Her nostrils flared as she took three steps back.

"I don't know how you're ever going to forgive me." With a rush of words, Joze continued, "I know I don't deserve it, but please—I'm begging you to forgive me."

Her mouth dropped open and she couldn't look him in the eyes anymore. She wanted to drop-kick him. "I told you. You should've believed me."

"You're right. You are," he spoke fast. "I can't believe I am such an idiot."

She wanted to scream at him, pummel him, something. But forgive him? No.

Shock shuddered through her. "All this time—"

"I wasted it. It's all my fault. But please—I want to make it right. Whatever it takes," he implored her with open arms.

"How can you?" Rage replaced the shock once again.

"I'll take you to the police. You should file a report against him. I want to kill him right now too."

I can't believe this.

"I'm begging you. Please, let's work this out. I'll do anything."

She melted a fraction and didn't manage to avoid his begging eyes. Then he moved. Was he going to drop to his knees?

Just then, his knees bent and touched the floor. "Don't leave me now. We've come so far these past days."

"Get up. Don't do that." How could she resist such a pitiful look? But he'd ruined everything they could've had. "Trust is paramount. You destroyed it."

She crossed her arms tight against her chest. What should she do? Everything warred in her. He wanted to make amends, but could she? Why should she? She didn't need him. "It's going to take more than you begging to fix this," she sputtered.

"It doesn't make sense now, but Todd was my best friend. Since we were babies. I never thought he was capable of such—base behavior. Not until you, and this week, and…"

The need to knock him over hit her between the shoulders, but she restrained the urge. "And I wasn't important enough for you to believe?"

His hands went to his head.

"Get up. Please." She couldn't see him on the floor any longer.

"Not until you forgive me."

With that, Maddie strode over to him and grabbed his arm. "Really."

How could he expect her to forgive just like that? Because of his God beliefs?

His hands caught and pulled her down in front of him. "What can I do?"

Her temper dropped a notch even though she struggled to free herself. "Nothing." Was it too late? Or was she holding on to the past too hard? "Now, let go."

He exercised his jaw. "I won't let it go this time."

Maddie stopped struggling. Why did he insist on pulling her so close? She didn't want him touching her right now.

He implored her with his eyes.

Too many years of hating that he didn't believe her began to dissolve a fraction. She pushed away from Joze and moved fast to keep him from seizing her again.

He pushed off the floor, looking so pitiful, she

almost wanted to say she would forgive him so he'd stop. What should she do? She needed him right now, as hard as it was to admit. But after the perp was caught, she'd leave Joze in the dust.

Plunking into the office chair, Maddie regarded him. No, she couldn't. It wasn't right to use him like that.

As much as she didn't want to admit it, something in her kept crying "forgive."

This time he kept his distance as he wiped his hands on his jeans. "I can't leave you in this mess. At least let me help you get your stalker arrested. Then we can worry about abandoning each other."

Maddie groaned. Was he trying to make light of the present situation? She tilted her head and studied him. "OK. But keep your distance."

"For now."

A huff died in her throat when she saw how serious he was.

30

How much more emotional upheaval could Maddie take? Aunt Lonna's office closed in on her as Joze used his feet to roll a couple inches closer. "You want me to retell the same Todd story? Again?"

"I know it's painful, but can you? Every detail. We have to go to the police about this, and I want to be armed."

"Well, I'm not dealing with this until we've closed out the drama at hand."

"OK, I understand."

Maddie wiped her eyes. She recounted the beginning of the story as she had the other night, but this time Joze was asking for more. Details she'd avoided.

Sucking in a breath, Maddie stopped. How to word it? "We were by the lake. Todd wanted to go for a walk and we took the one trail that leads to the top of the mountain. It was so quiet. I don't even remember hearing birds as we walked. We hadn't seen anyone on the trail in a good hour when he suddenly veered off the path. You know, I still don't know why I didn't get that sense of foreboding people talk about, but I didn't." She dropped her gaze to her hands. "I guess I trusted him too much."

Bending forward, Joze put his forearms on his thighs. "Go on."

Once again, he was a bit too close for comfort. Personal space must not mean anything to him. She gathered her strength. "He, he pulled me to some bushes. At first, I didn't get what was going on. But then, in a second, his eyes blackened." She sniffed. "And then I knew it was really bad…and no one was around to hear or to stop him. I knew I had to do whatever I could to get out of there, so I managed somehow to kick him…you know…before he could really do much. And I put everything I had into it. When he fell over…I moved as fast as I could and grabbed this thick branch on the ground and hit him in the chest as hard as I could. Then I took off.

"Good thing we drove my car. I got to the parking lot and left him on the mountain. And I didn't care if he ever made it back down."

"I'm sorry. I can't say it enough." He bit his lip. "He didn't have a scratch on him, you know? I thought if you'd hit him he'd have a bruise or something…"

She lifted her hand, palm out. How good it was to see belief in his face. "Maybe the stick only grazed him, I really don't know, but he didn't chase me."

The whites of Joze's eyes showed. Maddie reached for him. "You're not going to do something crazy, are you?"

His lips narrowed. "I can't promise you anything."

Now that he'd swung to her side, would he be as vicious against Todd? Did she want that? Maddie tucked her hair behind her ears. What if there were more victims? "What're you thinking?"

He seemed to consider saying one thing but instead said, "That's why you left school and didn't go back for a few years?"

This was hard stuff to talk about. "Yes."

Joze rubbed her arm. "I'm glad you did. And Todd never contacted you?"

"No."

They sat quietly a few more moments. Maddie pressed her lips together and studied him. Was he thinking the same thoughts?

She blew out a breath and pushed away the circle of thoughts.

Dread began to build again. Dread that another attacker was only feet away, waiting to pounce on her. And this time she might not make it out so unscathed.

As if he felt it too, Joze scanned the room. "I'm not losing you to another criminal. Let's get this room finished. We have to figure things out."

It occurred to her that he should've been at work. "What about your job? I didn't even think about it until now."

"Don't worry. I called my boss. He says I have to make it up to him, but he gave me a few days off."

"How much do you work?" She spun the chair around.

"Usually, two twenty-four-hour shifts. Sometimes three. Depends."

She slipped and put her hand out to right herself. Some papers had fallen between the wall and the desk. Maddie reached down and tried to get ahold of them, but they were too far back. Joze helped her pull the desk away, and she yanked the papers free. They studied them one by one.

Maddie dropped her shoulders and groaned. Nothing.

An hour later all the papers were off the floor and in some semblance of order by subject matter. The potential of finding nothing was great at this point.

Maddie knocked her fist against the table. Why couldn't Providence help her for once? She paused. If she didn't believe in God, how could she expect Him to do anything for her? Maybe Joze could do some praying and get help. She opened her mouth to ask, when something scraped against the floor. Turning, Maddie walked toward Joze who'd picked up a filing cabinet drawer and pushed it into place. "Is it empty?"

He slid the drawers open. A few file folders managed to stay in with some papers. They pulled them out and read through them. Only more invoice slips.

Maddie ran her hands along the bottoms of each drawer then shoved the last one closed. She needed a potty break. "I'll be right back."

In the corner of the room was a bathroom, the one amenity Aunt Lonna had insisted on having installed. Maddie closed the door.

Joze's muffled voice sounded through the thin door. "Please, God, we need some divine intervention. Help us find what we need to solve this thing."

Ha. Like God would just hand them evidence.

No toilet paper. She shuffled around and opened the bottom cabinet under the sink. The last roll sat to the side. As she took it out and went to put it on the holder it wouldn't fit. With growing impatience, she shoved it on the springy cylinder and something from the toilet paper roll popped into her hand. In an instant, she leaped back and almost dropped it in the toilet.

A flash drive. "Joze." She drew out his name.

Whoa, had God done that? Now she didn't know what to think.

His footsteps resonated. "What's happened?" No

fear in his voice.

She flung the door open. "I *found* a flash drive."

He raked a hand through his dark hair and smiled. "Good hiding place. But—is it the one we're looking for?"

31

Joze had been praying. Hard. "Forgive me" and "Help us now" type stuff. And now they had something. He lifted his hands to the sky. "Thank you, Lord."

Maddie strode to the stairs. "You think He's responsible?" She eyed him. "Let's go find out what's on it."

When was she ever going to come around and believe God was real?

He followed her to the house and waited while Maddie hurried to her room.

With her laptop on the coffee table, they scrunched together and pulled up the files from the thumb drive. It had only three files on it. Maddie clicked on the first. It was a series of pictures of a house. The last one showed a man walking up the walkway to the front door. Most of them were blurry as if the photographer had been in motion when the pictures were snapped. Even in the last one, the guy must've been walking away fast because they could only make out his brown jacket.

"It's the back of his head. Doesn't help us much." He drew closer to the screen. "Hey, that looks like the same brown jacket I saw on the guy who…" He hadn't told her about his attacks.

Maddie cocked her head. "Go on."

He raised his hand. Then he lowered it again. Since they were putting things out in the open, he might as well tell her. "Now, don't get mad, but I got attacked by some guy the other night."

She started to talk.

"Wait. I didn't keep it from you for any reason but that I didn't want you to worry."

Maddie fell against the cushions. "Again? I'm so sorry for bringing you into this mess."

"I must be making his job harder."

"You should've told me," she hissed.

"No way. You had enough to deal with. You didn't need to add me to your list. Besides I can handle myself."

She crossed her arms and scowled. "So, he has his two worst enemies all in one place. That'll make it easy for him."

"Don't be like that." He wanted to grab Maddie and pull her close but restrained himself.

"Do you see the logo on the back of the jacket?"

His hands itched to touch her again even though they had kind of an understanding. It wouldn't do to get her on the wrong side so soon. "Please let it be something that'll help us." He took a hard look. "I don't know what it is, do you?"

She ran to the kitchen and came back with a piece of paper. "I'll copy it down. I bet there's some way to do a logo search."

Joze waited for her to finish, the whole time bouncing his knee up and down. He was dying to see what else was on the drive. "What's in the other two folders?"

They scanned through them. Maddie stopped on one of them. "Look. A list of times."

"Hmm. But no reference as to what they refer to."

They moved on to the next document. Several addresses and pictures of the places filled a few pages. "Your aunt did some real surveillance. And these aren't the same places she printed in the journal. One's even in Massachusetts."

Maddie scratched her cheek. "She threw herself into whatever she believed in."

He took over the computer on the last folder. When he clicked it, he waited for it to load. A photo of RoRo and some doctor in a white coat jumped out at them. RoRo's head covered most of the guy's face, but he had the same brown hair as the first photo. Joze did a fist pump in the air. Oh yeah. They were so close to finding this guy he could almost taste it. "There's your proof. She got a picture of them together. And I bet that's why he trashed the place. He knows it exists."

He couldn't help himself. Joze got up and did a little dance. "And a doctor of all people. I wonder if he was selling illegal prescriptions to RoRo's gang. That's why I didn't want you to deal with him. See? If he knew what you were really after, who knows what he'd have done to you." He took a closer look. "I think I see a slip of paper passing between them."

Maddie blew out her cheeks. "The police should be brought into this. I'm calling Tuttle."

His gaze moved from her to the computer. "But...they won't see the significance. There are no drugs or anything shown in the picture. What can they do?"

She stopped. "Right. But what about at least telling them someone stole the journal?"

"We should." When he sat back down, Joze leaned against her. "We can check out those addresses."

Maddie didn't jerk away as he'd anticipated. *Good.* Things might swing in his favor. She wrote them down, took out the drive, and then hopped up. "I'm already gone."

They used the GPS on her phone to find the first one. True to the picture, the building was in a little better neighborhood. Joze clamped a hand on her arm. "Don't even think about getting out here. I'll go knock on the door and ask the questions."

For once she didn't fight him. He took cautious steps to the door and knocked. After another attempt and no one answering, he returned to the car.

She made as if to get out. "You could've knocked again."

"They aren't answering either way. They probably think I'm a cop."

Maddie sat back down. "Fine. But we'll have to come back later."

They headed to the second address. The photo had shown a brick building. When he pulled in, Joze read the sign. "The Reinhold Group. Looks like another doctor's office, don't you think?"

She agreed and got out. "Why in the world wouldn't Aunt Lonna give us some names?"

He leaned against the car beside her. "I guess she might not have known his real name." He scoped the building again. "It's worth seeing if any of the doctors' names start with a 'K'."

They entered the building, not quite as posh as the first one and not quite as clean. They stopped at the receptionist's desk in the hall. Joze tried not to breathe in the odor of human waste. Was a pipe broken somewhere? Formica counters instead of stone ones encircled her. A woman in her mid-fifties, her roots showing gray, greeted them. He took the lead. "Ma'am, do you have a list of the doctors in this office?"

She smiled up at him and drew out a pamphlet. "Here you go." Spitting out a bunch of names, she pointed as she talked. "But skip this one. He's no longer with us." She glanced down at the paper again. "Oh, and neither is this one or this one."

She said the names so fast he missed half of them.

Maddie leaned into his arm to see the pamphlet. Oh, how he craved her closeness. "Thank you."

The receptionist returned to typing something on her computer after giving them another dazzling smile. He sent a praise to the heavens. Pictures accompanied all the doctor's names and fields of expertise.

Maddie tittered. "I can't believe our luck."

"Not luck."

"Whatever."

How could she not see the divine intervention in all the things that'd happened? They moved out of earshot of the secretary.

Joze's finger traced down the page. First page, no 'K'. The same for the second and third. He flipped it to the back and stopped. "Look. Dr. Kilanti Bobritti."

They both looked hard at it. Maddie shook her head. "No. He's Indian. The guy in our photo has medium-brown hair."

"And he's older," Joze interjected. He dropped his hand to his side in frustration. What now? "You think there could be a doctor or two who are new or who were here too brief a time to get added to the list?"

She shrugged. "Very possible."

"Back to the receptionist." They returned to the counter. "Ma'am, could you tell us if there are any new doctors here?"

The woman narrowed her eyes.

Quick, come up with a reason. Without lying. "We heard about someone in this office, and I'd recognize the name if I heard it."

It took a minute to respond. "Could it be Dr. Laura Brick?" He shook his head. "OK, Dr. Paul Sherburg? Those are the only two new ones."

"No. Not that one either. It's a male. Medium brown hair. How about any doctors no longer with the practice? Maybe they weren't here long enough to get the photo done."

She returned to her computer and scanned it.

Maddie elbowed him and smiled.

"There was a Dr. Keith Adcock, but he's been gone for months."

Joze wanted to spike a pretend football. Outstanding. They had a name...perhaps. He spelled out the name to make sure they had it right. She agreed. "No others?"

"Not that come to mind."

They thanked her and hurried to the car. Maddie hurdled into him. "I'm leaning toward trusting God after all this. Wow."

He almost fell over. Miracle number three today. God was good. But the doctor could be a false lead. He didn't want to break the news that it might not be the man they were looking for.

Joze had an idea. "Put Keith Adcock into a search engine."

Maddie typed in the name and the buffer signaled the phone was working to retrieve the information. A different address came up for yet another office. Joze started the engine. "This guy knows how to move.

Let's try that one too."

32

The fragrance of hot asphalt and exhaust filtered through Maddie's window as Joze zoomed to West Hartford, and her stomach dropped with every mile that went by. This next doctors' office had to be the one. Dr. Keith Adcock was the best lead they had so far. But if it was him, they were stepping into his territory. "I don't know about this, Joze. I've got a bad feeling."

He sped through a yellow light. "We'll be careful."

She balled her fists together and tried to push away the tension growing in her shoulders. The mall came into view. Shoppers came and went with bags in their hands. Traffic picked up. They took a left and then another left. The New Britain Hospital towered to her right until they passed it. Two blocks later, they drove into a full parking lot.

Joze had trouble finding a space. It must be prime time when all the kids got out of school. Moms and tots strolled to the buildings. Maddie didn't get out as fast this time. She waited until Joze finally came around and opened her door. "Which building is it?"

He held out a warm hand and helped her out. Scanning the numbers, he checked each building and then pointed to one on the left.

She was being ridiculous. Maddie shook off the apprehension and linked her arm in Joze's. He gave her a funny look, but she ignored it and moved forward.

Keith Adcock. Stalker a la carte. And she was headed straight for him.

The sun cut into her vision, and she raised a hand to block it. As they entered, a couple of senior citizens held the door for them. Maddie took in the floor-to-ceiling glass walls that separated offices on each side from the hallway.

Joze pulled her to a directory on the wall. There he was. Dr. Adcock. Second floor. In an office with a bunch of other doctors.

She looked a minute too long. "What do we do if he sees us?" Her throat was so dry her tongue stuck to the roof of her mouth. "I mean—"

Joze guided her to the corner and put both hands on her arms. She tried to keep her focus on him and not what could happen. "Stay right at my side. I'll come up with something if he shows, OK?"

Why had she responded that way? Since when did she allow him to be so close? And to like it so much? She squirmed. They were moving too fast and she wasn't ready for it. First, they needed to rebuild trust if she was even going to think about letting him remain in her life. Maddie put a few more inches between them.

He didn't seem to notice her pull away as he focused on the steps in front of them. They took the stairs up to the second landing. "Wait."

Joze looked through the glass window in the door. "Just a long hallway. Come on."

Where was the tough woman in her now? Maddie managed to bolster herself some. She tilted her chin high and blew out a slow breath. "I'm fine."

He raised an eyebrow and guided her into the hall. People milled around from one door to another as Joze led her around the corner and entered the main hall. Once again floor-to-ceiling glass announced the entrances to each office. And then they were standing in front of the General Surgeon's doorway. Her eyes darted around.

Joze went straight to the receptionist inside. "Hello, is Dr. Adcock here today?"

The woman looked over the top of bright red reading glasses. "Do you have an appointment?"

"No."

She tapped the papers in her hand to straighten them. "He doesn't see walk-ins. You have to have an appointment."

Maddie checked the small counter that separated them from the reception desk. A few business cards sat in a clear holder. Must be all the associates. She pulled out Dr. Adcock's card.

Joze leaned toward the prim, middle-aged woman. "I'm looking for some information on him."

She pursed her lips. "What kind?"

"How long he's been here, how many years he's been a doctor. That sort of thing."

Her cold gaze never left him as she reached for a pamphlet. "Here's all you need to know about him."

He took it, and waved a thank you to her, and then guided Maddie over to the waiting area. At the furthest chairs, they sat facing away from the door and the receptionist. He opened it and held it between them. "Says he's been a doctor for twenty years. Hmm. Are we assuming your aunt and he hooked up because of the class reunion? That would make them the same age."

"Or within a year either way."

He harrumphed. "Must have finished school early by my calculations."

"I guess it's possible." They continued to read the sheet. "It doesn't say anything about all those other offices where he worked. Do you remember if they were the same type of doctor?"

It took him a second to respond. He flipped the paper over. "I'm not sure."

Maddie gasped at the picture on the back. "Look. He has the same brown hair."

"Did you see this guy at the funeral?"

She wrinkled her nose. "I don't know." What about all the other people who'd showed up at the dinner afterwards? Was he among the crowd? "It's scary to think he was in my house and I can't even remember seeing him."

"I doubt he came up and made a formal introduction. He probably kept to the outskirts of the party."

She nodded. "Let's get out of here. I think we got what we came for."

Joze ushered her to the door.

If it wasn't for the returning doom, Maddie would have hung back to ask the receptionist a few more questions, but she couldn't get out of there fast enough.

They hurried down the hall. A balding man in a white coat passed them, the sharp hint of antiseptic following him.

Maddie held her head up. Adcock wasn't bald. No worries. She told herself over and over to calm down. They were almost to the hall leading to the stairs again.

Joze reached for her hand and she held on tight.

People followed them down the hall. Now if they

could meld into the crowd, it'd be grand.

Maddie missed the 'wet floor' sign. One minute she was walking at a fast clip, and the next, her feet went out from under her. She reached for the wall, catching the side of her palm on the wainscoting and slitting her hand wide open. Searing pain shot through her hand. "Ow."

Joze tried to break her fall. She grasped his hand, smearing blood on his shirt with her other hand. Maddie stared at the red stain.

Several people gasped and stopped in mid-stride. One man missing his two front teeth tried to help Joze lift her off the ground. "Ma'am? Are you all right?"

"Uh, I think...so. We've got it. Thanks."

The man didn't look so sure as he moved away from them.

A couple other people stopped to ask if she was OK. She assured them she didn't need any other help. The sharp pain in her hand radiated up her arm.

Joze dropped to one knee and checked the wound, his gentle movements protecting her from further pain. Then his gaze shot over her left shoulder.

Maddie stiffened. "What is it?"

"Our guy is headed this way."

No way. Her body throttled into pure panic. She squashed herself against the wall as much as she could and whispered, "Let's get out of here. Now."

He helped her to her feet and put a hand around her waist. All the offices were open for anyone to see in the hall. Where could they go?

She looked right and left. A small hall led to the elevators. If Dr. Adcock was going that way, they'd be trapped.

Joze pushed her through a door several yards

away. Maddie tried to hold her breath and not cry out from the pain of knocking the injured hand on the doorframe.

He flipped the light on and locked the door. They were in a single bathroom.

"The family toilet?" She'd have laughed any other time. Bathrooms seemed to be their place of revelation lately.

"We're locked in and safe. And I can at least clean your hand in here."

True. Maddie looked down. A few drops of blood were at her feet on the tiny octagon tiles. Then she looked at his shirt and winced. "Sorry about your shirt."

Joze checked the spot. "I can get it out. Trust me, I've had worse on me and you really don't want to know about it."

Moving to the sink, Maddie took a few deep breaths. The sharp pain turned to stinging. "I believe you."

Joze turned the water on and helped her wash out the cut. "It might need stitches."

"No. I think it's fine." She eyed the door. The walls must be thick because she couldn't hear anything on the other side. Was Doc Adcock outside the door? Had he seen them? Her stomach dropped out like a load of rocks had been dumped into it.

"Well, I have Dermabond in my pack if need be." She frowned. "It's a surgical glue to keep the wound closed."

"Oh." Maddie returned her gaze to the door. "Did he see us?"

Joze slowed the winding of his arm as he wrapped her hand in paper towels. "I...don't...know." He scrunched his face. "Maybe?"

When he finished, he was able to tie the paper together. "That should hold for now. I have bandages in my car."

They both went to the door to listen. Maddie put her ear to the pine-colored wood and gently put her hand to her side. "How can we tell if he's there? I can't hear anything."

"I'll take a look." He opened the door a crack and then closed it. "I don't see anyone."

She moved close again. "But what if—"

A knock resounded through the little space and made her ears ring. Maddie jumped back and covered her mouth as a yelp escaped.

Joze lowered his voice like a lumberjack. "Someone's in here."

Her hands shook. Had he found them?

As if on an unconscious level, Joze got in front of her, his hand splayed on each side.

It was quiet again.

They waited.

One minute. Two. Three.

He relaxed his stance. "I need to take another look. Get ready to move out of here if I give the signal."

Her feet seemed glued to the spot. All she could do was nod.

He opened the door one inch. Then a little more. Then reached for her and took her good hand and dashed out.

So much for a signal. They stepped into a group of senior citizens a few doors down. They moved at a crawl to the elevators. Maddie tried to make herself as short as she could.

When the doors dinged opened, Joze pulled her to

the back of the elevator and wrapped his arms around her. It shielded her from all view. One guy whistled in their direction and grinned. Maddie could see only his sparkling eyes over Joze's shoulder. It took her a second to realize the elevator doors had closed and it began to descend. And it took a second longer to notice Joze's mouth nuzzling her neck. She widened her eyes. "Hey."

"Huh?" He stopped but didn't move away.

The doors dinged again and the crowd surged out. Joze strode to the exit and checked the hall to the main level. "Come on. I don't see him."

Maddie's pulse raced through her veins as they bolted to the car. She never wanted to be that close to the stalker again. "We're calling the police."

As they pulled out of the parking space, she looked over her shoulder. Outside the glass doors she spied a man in a white coat. She shook Joze's shoulder. "He's—there. He must've seen us."

Jerking the car into drive, Joze swung around. "I see him. Get down."

Maddie hadn't known it was possible to get on the highway so fast. *Please don't start crying*. "What are we going to do?"

"We're going to the police station."

33

How had Keith Adcock discovered them at the doctor's offices? Joze kept his eye on the rear-view mirror the whole way to the police station. This was unbelievable.

He checked Maddie for the hundredth time on the way into the station. She was failing at the tough look, and it made him want to pull her into his arms and tell her he'd do anything to protect her. Instead, he took her hand and squeezed it. "Hey, we've got this. Now we have a good idea who is after you and the police can progress in their investigation. It's going to be OK. We'll get a restraining order."

"They don't work." She must've heard horror stories about them too.

"I'm not leaving you."

"Do you think he'll follow me to college? I don't know what to do, Joze."

If only he had the answers. "We'll figure it out."

At the police station, Maddie dropped onto one of the hard waiting room chairs in the gray room. "I want this to be over. At this point, I'd set myself up as bait and let him come. I'm too tired to keep running."

He sat next to her. "No, you won't. Listen, calm down and think. We're here, and you've got backup."

He went to the window and avoided resting his hands on the darkened edge of the counter. He bet he could name a hundred different bacteria in that one spot. Boy, someone needed to get out some cleaning products. One of the officers he dealt with regularly headed into the tiny space behind the glass. "Hey, Brown. Is Officer Tuttle available?"

The officer behind the counter rubbed his bald head. "Evans. I thought you were on duty today."

"I had to take a few days off. How's it going?"

"Been a little quiet. I guess it's a good week for your vacation. They wouldn't be able to do it without you otherwise, man."

Joze grinned. "Oh, I'm sure Crozak has it covered."

Brown hooked his thumbs in his belt loops. "Jimmy boy? I don't know." He leaned in. "What're you doing down here if you're on vacation?"

"Need a little support. That's all."

"Let me check." He marched away.

It probably would've been a better idea to call first. Tuttle could be out on patrol or off duty.

He eyed Maddie. If she'd truly trust him, he could get somewhere, but she was still holding back. He didn't get it.

Joze pulled out his phone and tapped it to see the time. Then he parked himself beside Maddie, not quite touching the wall with his back.

Brown tramped out into the lobby. "He's on a call. He said to meet him at the Clare residence. Can I help with anything? Is it an emergency?"

Maddie stood and joined them. Officer Brown nodded in her direction. "Ma'am."

Should he bring another officer into the case? "No, but thanks."

They fist bumped each other. "See you around."

And he hoped he wouldn't regret that decision.

34

Where was Officer Tuttle?

Joze dropped onto Maddie's sofa and took one last look at her bandaged hand. He'd disinfected and rewrapped it. It took some Dermabond in the end to close up the wound.

He checked the grandfather clock in the corner again. Thirty minutes since they'd gotten back. That was forty-five minutes since they'd left the police station. He ran a hand through his hair. Why was he so edgy? He knew better than to think the police were even capable of running to every call. He'd been on the other side long enough to know his impatience was unwarranted. But still. The doctor saw them. He must know they were scoping him out. And now the danger level for Maddie was through the roof.

The doorbell chimed, and he bolted off the couch. "I'll get it."

Maddie wasn't far behind him. When he opened the door, Joze took a step back. "Hello?"

Two women smiled at both of them. Had he seen them at the funeral? What a terrible time for visitors. What if Officer Tuttle showed up while they were there? It'd be as awkward as when Mrs. Canney brought the food the other day and had most certainly seen them fighting.

Maddie stepped in front of him and he backed

away. "Can I help you?"

The shorter one folded her hands together over an orange dress that looked like a potato sack. "This may be a very bad time, but Mrs. Clare said we could pick up some paperwork Lonna had for the reunion. We're getting behind in our schedule and hoped you wouldn't mind if we stopped by for it."

The other one combed through her graying hair.

He glanced at her.

"That's right. We met at the funeral." Maddie ushered them in. She blinked hard. Every mention of her aunt seemed to warrant that response. He fought the urge to wrap his arm around her shoulder and pull her close.

The shorter one put out her hand. "Patty Wells."

Maddie took it, but her face remained blank. Was she still dwelling on her aunt?

The other lady sniffed and put out her hand. "Trisha Pord."

Maddie looked from one to the other. "Let me get them."

Joze followed on her heels. She put up a hand to stop him. "It'll only take a second. Why don't you seat them in the living room?"

He quirked an eyebrow. She obviously wasn't thinking. "No way. I'm going with you. Who knows if the doc is out there? He's had more than enough time to get here." He tried to keep the resentment out of his voice but failed. It wasn't any fun being on the other side of police and medical staff.

"That's true." She sighed, swiped a hand across her forehead, and then pivoted on her heel and returned to the foyer. "You two can be seated if you'd like."

The women scuttled into the living room and looked around as if it was the first time they'd been there, checking the antiques on the mantel and studying a few old photos on the wall.

Joze and Maddie went straight to the office. Joze's gaze darted over the yard and woods. On full alert, he checked the backside of the building before heading upstairs.

Maddie took the one pile of papers they'd set on the desk.

He studied every corner of the room. Had it only been yesterday he'd admitted to believing her about Todd? And where did they stand now? Once she came around, they'd worked together like a well-oiled machine. One that needed the other's input. Her ferocious care for her family was beginning to include him, too. He loved that about her.

How nice it would be to pull her close. He pushed back the dangerous thoughts. Right now, he needed to hyper focus on their surroundings.

Maddie cleared her throat. "You OK?"

Heat rose up his face. "Uh, yeah."

She moved closer, almost in the same spot as yesterday and he gulped.

Joze dropped the papers. He placed his hands on her shoulders and drew her closer. How good it was to have her in his embrace. And he had to touch her lips. He lowered his mouth to hers, not quite touching. Like the other night. But this time there were no interruptions. Would she let him kiss her?

She blinked. His breath picked up speed. And hers. He was so close.

Her eyes shined up to him. She seemed to be wrestling with want too. "Joze."

"Maddie," his response was soft.

Her hand went to his chest, and his heart beat strong against it.

He stayed just close enough. "We've wasted so much time."

Maddie narrowed her eyes, but he continued, "Not here. I—I mean since the incident."

"Those two ladies. We have to get back to them."

She tried to leave, but he pulled her back. "Wait."

He could almost taste her lips. And then his mouth was on her hot and moist yet soft mouth.

Maddie stiffened, but he pulled her closer until she yielded.

"Please forgive me," he said.

"I don't know." But she didn't back away.

So many emotions clogged his thinking. He should stop, keep a level head while the stalker remained on the loose. But his body refused.

"We need to get downstairs before they wonder what happened."

Good common sense. He loosed his grip on her, but she continued to look into his eyes. He knew he couldn't let her return to her old life without him.

Maddie put a hand to her cheek. "Come on."

He stayed put. "Say you feel the same as I do."

She looked down. With distracted movements, she scooped up the papers he'd dropped.

Fine. He could wait. For her.

When she stood, she touched his arm. "Later, OK?"

Just as he thought she was about to reach up to touch his lips, she laughed and moved away. "Later."

Sure. He fought the desire to ignore her comment and yank her into a tight embrace. How did she have so much restraint? And why couldn't she admit she felt the same way he did? He could see it in her eyes.

They locked the door behind them and took the papers to the women, but his eyes were only on her the whole way and not the yard and road where they should've been. Maddie sifted through them one last time. "I hope what you're looking for is in there. I don't know of any other forms pertaining to the reunion."

Patty took them and flipped through the pile. "Here's the main one we need. Look Trisha."

Trisha peered over Patty's shoulder. "Yes ma'am."

With a wave, Patty went to the door. "Thank you so much for taking the time to see us." She paused, her hand on the door. "Isn't it sad how your Aunt Lonna finally found love again and now she's gone. Just when she was starting over. And the soap business…."

Maddie grasped Joze's arm and pressed close to him. "Do you know who that person was?"

Hadn't they already figured out it was the doc? He gave her a questioning look.

Trisha screwed up her face. "She didn't tell you? It was Robert Adcock."

Whoa, whoa, whoa. Who was that? They'd found Keith Adcock not a Robert Adcock. "Do you mean Keith Adcock?"

Both women frowned and Patty said, "No. Robert. We went to school with him."

Maddie tightened her hands into a knot. "Is Robert Keith's middle name by chance?"

"We don't think so. His middle initial in the year book was a B. I remember because I was writing up the now and then photo forms for the photography company only last week. But I think he may've had an older brother."

Joze held the door for them. Dusk crept across the porch. "Well, thanks for the information."

Maddie yanked him into the living room. "What in the world? I'm confused."

Not more than him. "Two men with the same last name? It's got to be part of the fraud your aunt was checking out."

She froze. "My aunt would've known if the guy wasn't the same man she went to school with."

He stroked his chin and paced the floor. "What if they're related and look a lot alike? Hence the reason she didn't pick up on the difference. It has been what...thirty years? It's a long time and plenty of people change after high school."

With a glimpse out the window, Joze noted the street lights blinking along the street. The almost dark was always so hard to see into with the gray filtration of dark and light mixed. He moved to the side window and squinted to see into the woods. Where was Tuttle? Energy pulsed through his veins making it hard to sit still. The sooner all this was over, the better.

Maddie tinkered around in the living room, looking as nervous as he was. She fluffed pillows, moved a set of books several times, and even pushed the rug an inch with her foot to straighten it.

They'd missed lunch and his stomach growled. "I'm calling the officer again. It's been way too long." He pulled out his cell phone. "I keep forgetting I don't have his number."

"You want me to call him?"

It might be better considering she was the victim. "Go ahead."

He planted himself beside her and tried to listen through the other side of her phone. The voice on the other end came through clear. "Miss Clare, I'm on my way."

Joze nodded at her. Maddie replied, "See you soon."

When she hung up, Joze helped her off the couch. "Think we can get something to eat afterward? I'm starving."

"Sounds good to me." Maddie brushed her hands through her hair and pulled at her shirt.

"You look fine. Make sure you have the flash drive. I need to use the boys' room. I'll be right back."

"Oh, sure. Sorry if I forgot to put a clean towel in there to dry your hands."

He shooed away her worry.

Five minutes later, Joze treaded down the hall. Why was the house so quiet? Deadly quiet. "Maddie?"

No answer.

Blood rushed to his head, and his heart pounded. Dread filled his gut. "Maddie. Where are you?"

Only silence answered.

35

Dirt and leaves filled Maddie's mouth as she struggled against the hard grip of the man pinning her down, her face to the ground. Earthy decay filled her nostrils. She tried to scream, but he smashed her even harder into the loose soil, sending mud up her nose. She kicked and flailed against his body that pinned her, but her zip-tied wrists made it impossible to get her bearings. Why had she opened the front door? All she had to do was wait for Joze to return. He wouldn't have fallen for the costume police hat. Tears burned the corners of her eyes.

Something overhead creaked, and the man flipped her over and pointed the long barrel of a gun toward the slats of the porch above.

The front door opened and Joze rushed out. He was talking, almost yelling into his cell, "She's gone."

Using her eyes, she pleaded with the man. *Please don't shoot him.*

Dr. Adcock nodded toward Joze. The street light barely reached through the lattice work along the bottom of the porch, but she got his meaning.

As the stairs groaned, Joze's boots clumped down them and his voice grew quieter as he headed to the woods.

Keith heaved her toward the tiny section of loose lattice work where he'd dragged her in. "Don't say a word."

She nodded, eyes big.

At the opening, he pushed her out and half-dragged her to the neighbor's driveway. She scanned the yard. All lights were out and no cars were in the drive. Just as she was about to scream, he guessed her thoughts and threw his arms around her neck and over her mouth, pulling a few strands of hair out. She swallowed a squeal. Her nose burned from the dirt forced in when her face slammed into the ground. She tried not to breathe too deeply. The burning was bad enough.

He yanked her around to the backyard and shoved her against the corner of the old Victorian house. After surveying the area, he forced her across the grass and through two more yards, and then cut along the side path to the front of Mr. Conner's house.

The tan sedan waited in the empty drive. Bile filled her mouth. He threaded his hand through her tied arms and opened the trunk, setting her off balance. She struggled to remain upright. Numbness threatened to overtake her mind. *No.* She needed to take in everything, but her body began to give in to the terror permeating her being.

"No. Please."

The gun went to her head. "Get in."

Maddie pulled back, shaking her head.

"Now. Or I'll hog tie you."

She clambered over the bumper and into the trunk. He threw the hat in beside her. The door clanked close and encased her in dank darkness as black as a quagmire. Her sobs echoed in the little space.

Streetlights flooded in a second later. She breathed in fresh air and relief. Had Joze found her and stopped the doctor?

A man towered over her. She squinted to see him, but he blocked out the light and his shadow covered him. He was too tall to be Joze. Maddie cried out. The doctor stuffed a cloth into her mouth. Maddie gagged and tried to move her head away, but he wrenched a clump of her hair back and held her tight while he shoved it in a bit more. The roots of her head stung.

And the door closed again.

Maddie tried not to gag and throw up. She didn't want to die like this.

The car reversed and threw her into the metal framework. Her head pounded against the wheel well, surging pain like lightning across her skull.

It hurt to do anything, but she had to stay vigilant. *Think.* What direction was he going? She tried to keep up with his turns but there were so many she couldn't. With her hands tied behind her back, Maddie couldn't reach anything except the wires to the speaker system. She pulled as hard as possible. One by one they gave.

The car squealed to a stop. How long had they been on the road? Not more than thirty minutes.

The trunk door slid open again. This time all she saw was a huge metal flashlight as the doctor swung it through the air and at her head.

36

Officer Tuttle pulled up to the Clare house beside Joze, who paced a hole in the front yard. He yelled, "Where have you been?"

The officer's hands went up. "Calm down. Four squads are on their way. Now tell me what happened."

With all the strength he could muster, Joze thrust his hands to his side and not across the officer's face the way he wanted to. "I left her alone for five minutes. That's all. The alarm was on. Everything was locked up. And when I came out, Maddie was gone."

He went back to pacing, waving his hands as he spoke. "Do something now."

The officer marched to the side yard, flashlight out and hand on weapon.

"I already checked the woods, the backyard, across the street."

More light began to bounce around the trees as more cruisers pulled up. Brown climbed out of the second car. "You OK, Evans?"

He nodded. "Please, he took her. Robert Adcock. It has to be him. He saw us at his office today. Well, he goes by Keith."

Tuttle was back. "Slow down. Who's that and what's his connection to Madeline Clare?"

Joze relayed all the evidence they'd discovered and how they were on their way to report the incident that had happened at the doctor's office when Maddie simply disappeared.

More officers arrived. Joze waved to the crew he'd worked with for three years. A couple slapped him on the back. "He's been stalking her since Thursday. You know, Tuttle, because we've had to call you a few times."

"Let us search the neighborhood." Brown instructed the officers and drove off.

All the men scattered, combing the streets.

Joze wrenched his hair in his hands. Not Maddie. After all the work he'd done to keep her safe. "Please, God, protect her. Let us find her. Direct us. I don't know where to look."

His head popped up from his prayer stance on the steps. The flash drive. It had an address in Massachusetts. The only one they hadn't driven to. And, of course, the house where no one answered the door. Two possibilities.

And then he plummeted back into despair. Maddie had the flash drive. Which meant Keith Adcock had all their evidence.

He had to call Maddie's mom. Why hadn't he thought to do it already? He ran through the house and into the kitchen. Everyone had an emergency number list. He searched the fridge and found it on the side. Dialing her number, he waited ten agonizing seconds for her to pick up. "Ma'am, this is Joze. Your daughter has been kidnapped."

37

Maddie sucked in the stale, dead air around her as she stirred, the low pitch of rumbling coming from a roadway.

Where was she?

One eye opened. Panic radiated. She wasn't at college in her dorm. She was in a small, dark trunk. Screams fought to escape but died on the gag in her mouth.

She was going to die. The knowledge sent her into motion, kicking the sides of the car, even with the searing pain in her head. Her hand ached where the plastic cuffs had chafed the laceration on her palm. She cried and thrashed but the car didn't stop. The hood didn't pop open from her angry beating this time.

Some of the gag hung out of her mouth leaving it a little loose. She worked it with her tongue until it loosened bit by bit. Good thing he hadn't checked to see how much he'd stuffed in. With one final thrust of her tongue, the bulk of it fell out and she blew as hard as she could until it shot out of her mouth.

At last the car slowed and then stopped. She grew still. Was it possible to get in a stooped position where she could hurtle herself at him when he opened the trunk?

Good thing he hadn't tied her feet together. She rolled to her stomach and scrunched her knees up as best she could.

Shuffling came closer.

With as much balance as she could muster, Maddie used her aching head to help get her body in the right position to lurch out as soon as the trunk door opened.

The key scratched in the lock.

Maddie counted in an effort to calm her outraged limbs.

The trunk popped open and she vaulted out with all the might she could muster. Her body crashed into his, sending him flying backwards.

Doctor Adcock cried out as he landed on his back.

Maddie hit the ground so hard it took her breath. She gulped in air as she shot to her feet and took off. *Don't look back like all those dumb movie chicks.* A huge yard with manicured gardens flowed down a small mountain. Trees surrounded the property from where she could see. They were her best bet. Maddie worked to stay upright without the use of her hands as she ran. She fought the pain but couldn't stop the tears.

Something wet trickled down her temple. The flashlight must've done a number on her head and the pounding proved how hard he hit her.

The tree line grew closer, but it was still so far away. Don't give up. Don't die out here. Keep going.

In the next second, her attacker lunged forward and pushed her so hard she stumbled and lost her balance. She tried to ball up to absorb the fall, but her head pummeled the ground.

Everything went black in a daze of pain.

38

Joze wanted to be moving, searching, anything but standing here doing nothing. Tuttle and Brown stood in front him as the cool night air dampened the ground and everything it touched, including him. He rubbed at his moist shirt.

Brown spoke for Tuttle. "We have a K-9 unit on the way. But they're coming from Hartford. Be patient."

Joze couldn't take hearing those words one more time. He walked away to temper the building anger. Patience was an impossibility when the woman he loved was in the hands of a potential killer.

He loved her? Truth was, he'd never stopped. He'd hidden it under self-righteousness and a sense of loyalty to Todd, but it had been there all the time. Why did it have to take this nightmare to bring him around? All the wonderful things about Maddie clouded his mind. He went back into prayer mode. *God be merciful.*

Returning to them, he took out his phone. Weren't some of the addresses Maddie and he'd visited on his phone? He pulled up his GPS history and found one of them. "Guys, here's the address to one of the offices we visited."

Brown took the phone out of his hand and Tuttle wrote down the address.

He folded his arms together. "The other one was

those office buildings past New Britain Hospital. Um," he snapped his fingers, "Twenty-nine, ninety-five New Britain Way. Yeah, that's the other address. It's the one Doctor Keith Adcock works at." They copied down what he said. "Oh, and there was a house a few blocks past Rusk Street on…Applegate, I think. It could be related to the doctor." He shook out his hands as tingles of tension coursed through him. "And I already told you about Massachusetts. I don't know that one, but you can do a search on Adcock and Mass to see if there's a connection."

"We're on it." Tuttle called on his mic to send officers to the locations.

If he could only get in his car and figure it all out on the way he'd be gone, not sitting around helpless.

Mrs. Clare bowled into the driveway, sending exhaust and grass cuttings through the air.

He shrank back. How was he going to explain that he'd let her daughter fall into the hands of her stalker?

She stormed out of the vehicle and screamed, "Joseph Evans, this is all your fault—again."

39

Eyes flying open and body tensing, Maddie struggled and pulled her head back as far as she could until the gun appeared in her line of vision and returned to her temple. What had happened two seconds ago? A black haze and the doctor's voice were the last things she remembered.

The doctor pushed the barrel against her head so hard that it had to be leaving a divot in her skin. She stilled.

"Stand up and walk." He didn't mince words.

It took her a second to get her balance. Maddie looked from him to the house on the hill. A stately mansion occupied the top of the mountain. Where were they? Were these the Berkshires? This had to be the Massachusetts address. As long as she'd been conscious and aware of time passing it made the most sense.

He gave her a shove and she stumbled. "You don't need to be spying. Keep your eyes forward."

They walked down a hill away from the stone Victorian. Maddie kept her eyes on him as much as she could, but it took careful steps in the light of the flashlight to keep upright.

His posh suit didn't fit the surroundings or the violent abduction she'd just lived through. She eyed his wingtip shoes. Not good for mountain climbing.

Could she knock him off balance and gain some distance before he could aim the gun at her again?

He pulled his black trench coat a little tighter. "You know, I shouldn't have taken your aunt out. It was the one mistake I made. But what do you do? Nobody wants to be lonely the rest of their lives. But really this is her fault. You can blame her for why you're involved. I tried to stop her before she blabbered to you. It was just my luck that she died in that fluke plane crash." He sighed and shook his head. "But then that left you to take care of. And I only meant to warn you. Until you had to get that medic involved."

Maddie gasped. "She didn't tell me anything. All of this is because you attacked me at the carnival."

"Come on. She told me she tells you everything. Stop lying. It's too late to change things anyway."

Maddie avoided a stump as they drew within feet of the trees. She had to stop him. Once they entered the trees, no one would ever find her again. She slowed. Keep him talking. "You shouldn't have sold prescriptions illegally. Then my aunt wouldn't have been involved if she hadn't seen you dealing with a drug lord."

He snorted. "That was the least of my problems."

What did he mean? She stopped.

He dug his nails into her arm and thrust her further into the forest. She landed against something hard.

Doctor Adcock brushed off the surface beside her. He pulled a long metal bar through some latches, and a door sprung open at his touch.

What was this place? Her heart beat so hard it threatened to come out of her chest.

She squinted to see into the ink-black hole that opened up. She couldn't go in there. Maddie trembled, and it was difficult to take breaths. "No."

He set the gun down, yanked her to the hole, and then slit her handcuffs off. With the fastest swing she could muster, Maddie brought her hand around to make contact with his head, but he thrust her forward. She tumbled down and down until her feet hit solid ground and crumbled under her. "Ms. Clare, meet my brother, Keith. He didn't stay out of my business either."

Was someone in there with her? No movement shifted in the dark space. "But you're Keith."

He snorted. "Well, I am now."

He'd taken his brother's identity?

The door closed with a definitive clank.

40

Joze couldn't stop the panic any longer. The Hartford K-9 unit loaded their dogs into the back of their cruisers. Lights, neighbors, and bystanders covered the street in front of Maddie's house. He didn't wait for them to debrief the officer in charge of the case, but strode up to them. "What's going on? Did they get a lock on her scent?"

One of them raised an eyebrow and headed to Officer Tuttle. The other checked his gear and looked in on his shepherd. "Sir, we deal only with the officer in charge."

He threw his hands up and waded through the officers to Tuttle. "What's going on?"

It took Tuttle a moment to acknowledge him. "Listen, I need you to wait over there. Let me get the details first."

Not another stall tactic. Acid burned his stomach as he struggled to stay where the police had asked him to remain. With his pulse in overdrive and teeth grinding, Joze tried to make eye contact with any one of them across the yard. Couldn't they see how much he needed to know what was happening?

If he'd done this or that then she wouldn't be gone. But there really was no stopping Maddie from being her independent, tough self, either.

When he looked up, Mrs. Clare had moved to the

front porch on the top step. She needed comforting. Focus on her for now. He stopped at the bottom of the steps and drove down all the emotions welling in him. "Can I get you anything? A blanket? A drink of water?"

She didn't look up. Maddie got her hard exterior from this woman for sure. "I'm fine."

It didn't look that way. He teetered between leaving her alone and pushing her to talk. "They're going to find her. I've worked with a lot of these men, and they won't stop until they do, Mrs. Clare."

A sniffle escaped her. "This is my fault. I tried to blame you—for this—for what happened four years ago, but I'm not going to do it anymore. I don't want the past to take a slice of my life away any longer. If I'd been there for her, this would've never happened. She's a grown woman and I've been treating her like I did when she was young." For the first time she looked him in the eye. "Maddie was trying to tell me something. But I didn't listen." She wiped her sleeve across her eyes. "I…never listen."

"I know people always say don't blame yourself. And I get how impossible that is right now, but you really shouldn't. We have to get through this." If he could just listen to his own words and stop circling blame around himself. All the anger drained out of him and left weariness. "This is all on me. I'd never leave her unprotected. The alarm was set and everything. I just never guessed she'd open the door to that doctor." He stopped, conflicted. "None of this makes any sense. Why'd she do it? If I could, I'd do anything to go back and stop her. But—"

She pulled her hair back and rested her elbows on her knees. "I might not ever get a chance to fix things."

Without a thought, he headed to her side and sat down. "Don't say that. We're going to find her. I won't stop until we do. And she's going to be so glad to see you it won't matter anymore."

Mrs. Clare rolled her head forward and started to sob. Joze put his arm around her, and she didn't resist. How was he ever going to make it up to her?

Being helpless stripped him bare. This was what God had been trying to tell him. The one thing that Joze knew but couldn't let go of. He wasn't in control. He needed to leave it to God. *God, be Maddie's hero from here on out. Save her before it's too late.*

41

Something decaying permeated the atmosphere around Maddie, leaving its odor draped around her like a moth-eaten wool blanket. Her hardness had worn away as she'd reverted to the helpless teenager after Todd had attacked her. She struggled to control the old guilt that worked its way into every pore—guilt that this was all her fault. She deserved it.

"Help." She sat balled up against an unseen corner, battling the past, shaking so hard she thought she might vomit. The cry wasn't loud enough to be heard by someone even standing close, but her throat burned so bad it stole any chance for a real outcry.

Where was she? If she'd tried harder, she'd be able to guess. But she'd given in. Like after the incident when she'd left college and didn't return.

Then she remembered. Massachusetts. This had to be the house in Massachusetts. Too many bumps on her head was addling her thoughts.

The smell continued to waft up her nostrils. Maddie buried her head in her arms. There was no time to give up. She had to find something, some way to get out.

And she had to figure out what was causing the awful smell. Sucking in a couple breaths through her mouth, Maddie managed to slow some of the shaking. If she got up and moved around, it'd help, for sure. She forced herself onto her knees and breathed again. Reaching out her hand, she touched the rough wall of cement. *Please don't let any bugs run across my fingers.*

A leafy vine tickled her palm. The room must not be sealed. A new panic filled her. That meant water could get in. Was it possible to drown out here? She struggled off the ground. *Please don't let it start raining.*

Her head bumped the low ceiling. Was it about a four-foot-high area? She pressed her back up and measured. Maybe almost five feet but no more.

With a careful step, Maddie put one hand on the wall and thrust the other one out. One slow step at a time, she shuffled forward as best she could. Her foot thumped against an unyielding object.

With quivering hands, she lowered herself bit by bit and lightly touched it. Material. Moist, sticky linen. She slid her hand around the object and realized it connected to something. Her fingers moved downward. Waxed laces.

The next second, she hurtled backward. It wasn't something. It was someone.

And she'd touched the source of the decaying stench.

42

Joze couldn't believe this was real and not a nightmare he couldn't wake from. The news splashed Maddie's kidnapping story across every television screen in New England.

By Tuesday morning not even the K-9 unit had found anything other than their exit point several houses down from the Clare residence. He must've been in the dark woods when her kidnapper sped off with her. Torrential rain pelted the window of his little kitchen where he sat chugging a bowl of cereal that he couldn't taste.

Three days. *Three long* days and still nothing.

He'd donned his EMT uniform. Today he'd hit the road and search with his buddies. They'd take every lead they could come up with. And he had to be ready if she was hurt…or worse.

The police hadn't found Dr. Adcock's personal residence yet. But it had to be a matter of time. With the Internet, no one was ever really anonymous.

His police scanner went off. Joze jerked up. What was that about a dead body? The scanner came to life again. "A DB. Male." He dropped his shoulders and sent a thank you to God. The voice continued over the static. "Cause unknown at present. All units report."

The dispatcher gave an address.

He couldn't finish the last few bites. His cell phone

rang and he slid the answer button to the right. "Hello?"

Beaucamp answered. "You're going to want to answer that call."

"The one the scanner just put out?"

"Yep."

"On my way." Joze shot out of his chair. If his buddy wanted him there, he'd be there.

Joze maneuvered around stubborn motorists who didn't seem to get the importance of his tailgating. What if it was their loved one? He kept his growing cynicism at bay.

When he screeched to a stop on the road, he noted the policemen at the perimeter of a taped-off section. Some bystanders craned to see whatever they could. He hurried under the tape, stopped at the door, and then called, "It's Evans. Can I come in?"

"Give us a while," Brown yelled. "I'll send someone to let you in once the scene is processed. And don't forget to put on the booties at the door."

No. More waiting? "Just tell me who it is!"

"Give us a minute," came a muffled reply from down the hall.

He straightened up and tried to see down the long hall where the voice emanated from. Who was it and why did Beaucamp think he should be here?

He did as he was told even though he must look like a preschooler with a cupcake just out of reach. Joze took in the large home with upgraded crown molding and shiny hardwood floors.

It seemed hours later when Brown and Beaucamp came out of a back room and beckoned him down the hall. Joze hurried in, careful not to touch anything. "Come take a look. Is this your friend?"

Joze's heart beat a fast cadence. His nerves sent shock waves all the way to his fingertips.

He stopped in the doorway of the room where Brown had once again disappeared.

A man's body rested on the bed as if he'd been sitting up and had fallen over. Dr. Adcock. The room narrowed He moaned. "No." His hands went to his head. "That's Dr. Adcock but how are we going to find Maddie now?"

The pressure in his chest fought to be released.

Beaucamp held up a bagged piece of paper with gloved hands. "Says he was being persecuted by the police. We found prescription meds in unmarked bags. Several script notepads laying around from different offices. This guy was in some serious trouble."

Joze wanted to punch the wall. "Please tell me you found something leading to Maddie. I can't take it. I have to hear you say it."

Brown's head dropped. The other officers in the room looked away.

"I'm telling you, she's in Massachusetts. Get me the next of kin's address and I'll go myself." He barreled out of the house.

By the afternoon, Joze was beside himself. He waited by the scanner for any news that'd lead him to Maddie. His cell phone left pressure marks on his hand, but he refused to set it down in case Brown or David called.

He put his medical bag together and rechecked it half a dozen times. It may come down to him finding her. Alone.

It had been long enough. He had to get out and start his own search.

43

The slap of rain against the window beat in time to Joze's pounding heart. David Beaucamp sat across from him. What if Maddie lay out in the elements, hurt or bleeding? A cold front had blown in during the night and threatened to turn to an unusual, light snow. "What are we going to do if it snows?"

David thumped the table. "What can we do?"

The fact that his good friend sat across from him didn't help. He needed to be out searching. Why had David insisted he go in for a break anyway? Joze eyed him. "Wait a minute. You know something. I can see it."

His friend pushed back in his chair, legs spread wide in a deceptively easy stance. "OK—this isn't how I wanted to tell you, but...the Massachusetts state police went up to the next of kin and talked to them. His parents hadn't seen Dr. Adcock in over a year. They didn't know where he was or anything. When they broke it to them that he'd committed suicide, his parents didn't seem too shocked. Officer Torney said it was weird the way they didn't react appropriately." He got up and started a restless prowl around the room. "What parents don't cry when they hear their son has died?"

Joze got out of his chair too. The suspense killed him. "Get to the point, David."

His friend made a sharp turn and continued around Joze. "They said he'd had trouble all through school. Never had any friends. But he managed to get his doctorate." He turned again and headed back. "Last year, he had a big blowout fight with them."

David halted. "He never talked to them again."

"So they never heard whether his license was revoked or what happened?"

David raised his palm. "No."

"What about the fact that there were two Adcocks? Robert and Keith."

"They said their younger son was Robert. They hadn't heard from him in years."

Joze scratched his chin. So fraud wasn't part of the issue. "What kind of family never talks to each other?"

"A broken one." He plunked into his seat. "But guess what? I haven't gotten to the strange part yet."

Joze sat back down, too, and pinned his elbows on the table. He was going to hyperventilate if David didn't get to the point, and fast. "Go on."

"When they showed the couple the picture for identification, they said it wasn't Keith but Robert in the photo. Now, that got them worked up."

Joze leapt out of his seat. "You're saying the one brother took the identity of the other one? How? Why? We wondered about that very thing."

"My guess?" He studied Joze. "He had lost his license and was about to go to jail in Pennsylvania. I think he decided to get out of it all by becoming his brother. His brother was also a doctor, you know? Adcock then moved to Connecticut and started practicing at another medical office in Hartford where he wasn't known."

"That's the coldest thing I've ever heard." Joze

wiped his brow. "So where's the brother?"

"We haven't located him at present."

Joze got tingles. Not good. How did Maddie play into all this?

And what of the journal? "Maddie Clare's aunt must have figured it out. Between the pictures and addresses, she must've known that he wasn't who he said he was."

"We've factored that in. But we may never know how much she knew."

"Has anyone found her journal at his residence?"

David shrugged and stood. "I'd have to check with Brown to find out."

"It could clarify things."

Retrieving his hat, David stopped at the kitchen door. "I have to get back to duty. I'll call you if I hear anything else."

"Thanks, man."

Before his friend made it to the front door, Joze stopped him. "Hey, can I have the address to Adcock's parents?"

"Dude, I told you, they've already followed up every lead there."

"We have to stick together in this town. Please. I won't do anything dangerous." *Oh please, let the small town brotherhood code work this time.*

"It'll be my badge if you screw up."

Joze put his hand on David's shoulder. "I won't."

David hung his head. "You're going to have to find a way to accidentally see it on my paperwork."

With a whoop, Joze smacked his friend on the back. "I'll repay you. I promise."

44

Maddie wiped her hand on the floor for the hundredth time and tried not to let bile climb up her throat. How long had she been there? Her eyes still hadn't adjusted in the utter pit of blackness.

It was cold, so cold. She stood. "I don't want to freeze to death. Please," she yelled.

Defeat dared to take her breath.

She got back on her feet and took even smaller steps to the left until the same hard wall met her palm. Maybe eight feet across? She followed the wall straight ahead. Please don't let the body be sprawled in the same direction.

Something cushy padded under her feet. She bent down and ran her hand along something silky. A sleeping bag? If God was there, why had He provided a sleeping bag and not a rescue?

How many bugs infested the underside of it?

Past the sleeping bag, her touch reached some cans that were empty. Leaves and sticks lay on top.

Maddie returned to her corner and wept. She banged on the walls with her fists and pushed at the ceiling, scraping her knuckles on the sandpapery texture of her tomb. Her screams went unheard. The house was far away...but if someone was in the yard, maybe there was a chance they'd hear her. She couldn't give up.

The cold began to seep into her clothes. She'd had her jacket on before the knock on the door, but it wasn't her winter coat. And wherever she was, the temperature seemed to have plummeted.

No food or water. But at least she had the blanket if she needed it, which could be sooner than later. She pulled her legs tight against her abdomen and slumped to the floor. Her eyes fluttered. She couldn't keep them open.

Startling awake, frigid cold bit at her toes and fingers. How had she allowed herself to fall asleep? Maddie tucked her hands into her armpits and shivered. She'd have to get the sleeping bag, bugs and all.

The odor from across the small space had let up some. Must be from the cold.

With careful movements, she pulled the blanket and hoped the body wasn't resting on any part of it. It gave with little resistance. She cuddled under it and tried not to breathe in the moldy tang that encircled her from moving it. Her stomach grumbled with hunger pangs.

Just five minutes. It's all she needed to get the warmth back in her body. Then she'd go back to fighting against the forces that held her in.

She counted to keep her mind trained on anything but her current reality. With little strength left, Maddie stood and avoided bumping her head on the low ceiling. The room seemed to be like some sort of bunker. Could it have been built during the war?

She tried to hold the blanket around her with one hand, and managed to bang on what she thought was the hatch to the bunker. It gave way a millimeter and then clanked back down.

Her strength renewed, she gave it everything she had. Pushing and yelling, she smacked against the entrance over and over but the millimeter never became two or three.

All her power waned in a matter of minutes. The door wasn't going to open.

Maddie dropped to the ground and wailed. "Why, God? Why are You doing this to me? You never protected me. You were never there when I needed You."

Hot tears poured down her face and chilled in seconds. She balled up, ignoring the musty odor of mold.

When she opened her eyes again a tiny glint of gray filtered in. She blinked. Daylight? Slowly her vision adjusted. She could make out the form of the body. The size suggested it had to be a male, but the bit of light didn't reveal any more detail other than a white lab coat.

A doctor's coat? Was this Dr. Adcock's brother? He'd said his brother never stayed out of his business. Had it brought him to murder?

Panic welled up and took over. If he hadn't gotten out, how could she? She scratched at the walls and tore a nail loose. Was there a crevice...any other possible way out? The pain barely registered. She strained to control her brain but gave in to the fear instead.

Water began to seep down the wall. She darted her gaze to the tiny spot of light. Was that rain? She listened. The drip became a small steam.

Moments later, Maddie forced away the sheer panic and allowed reason to take over. "God, please get me out of here. Please."

Water inched to her feet.
It was hopeless.

45

How long could Joze hold his professional stare—the one that all medical personnel knew how to maintain when they didn't want people to know what they were really thinking—before he exploded? And why did it seem like every officer in the building was staring him down as he stormed down the hall on his way to David Beaucamp's desk?

He rounded the corner and spotted his friend a couple cubicles down. Plunking into the seat beside him, Joze blew out a breath. "Thanks for calling me in, David."

"Could you take a look at a sketch for me? Wait, let me find it."

Once again, Joze watched every cop swarming the precinct around him and played along with his friend. "Sure."

David put his hand on a paper file in front of his computer, and then got up to check something at the printer, his back turned. "So, have you witnessed anything suspicious since last night?"

"No, sir." Joze eyed the black folder and almost jumped out of his seat to throw a fist pump into the air. There it was, the address he'd begged for.

"Oh, here it is." He swung around and held out a paper.

Joze took it, and then handed it back. "That's close

to what I saw last night."

"Great. Thanks. Well then, have a nice day. Contact me immediately if you do get more information."

"I will."

Joze hightailed it out of the police station.

At his car, he pulled out his phone and tapped the address into the GPS app. Wait a minute. It was one of the addresses Lonna Selby had on her flash drive, he was almost certain.

There was no time to waste thinking about it. He had to go. Driving west, he headed to interstate ninety-one. This would be the quickest trip he'd ever taken to the state of Massachusetts.

Joze gunned the engine and swooped between two cars as he entered the highway. The rain made the road slippery and he had to fight the pull of the wheel as the car threatened to slide. "I'm coming, Maddie."

The traffic slowed and Joze went into beg mode. "God, get me there in time."

When cities faded away to hills and trees, Joze checked the GPS again. The blue line covering the interstate showed he was on track. An hour from now to get to his destination.

It spit out the next turn coming up in two miles. He grabbed it and put it back in the holder where he could see the front screen lit up with the map on it. All these years were gone in an instant. And Maddie was worth it.

His mind raced. Forty miles to his destination. What was he going to do when he got to the address? Would the people even talk to him? He didn't have a badge to flash at them or any authority, but his gut insisted that the Massachusetts location was the key to finding Maddie.

Rain drizzled against the windshield, and he turned his windshield wipers back up.

What if he found her but it was too late?

The list of items in his medical bag ticked through his mind for the gazillionth time. There was no AED machine to shock a person's heart. Please, God, don't let him need one.

The car in front of him braked hard and stopped. Why?

He tried to see around the growing line of cars. A few flashing lights left odd patterns because of the rain. Must be an accident. Any other time he'd pull over and help, but Maddie's life was at stake. Inching forward, he hovered over his wheel. An ambulance waited on the side of the road. Good. Help had already arrived.

How could he be so callous about the scene just out of view? Someone there could be in bad shape. But Maddie still hovered in every part of his mind. "Please move, cars. I gotta get out of here."

46

Two inches of water drove Maddie against the wall. There was no use in trying to avoid it any longer. The whole floor disappeared under it an hour ago, carrying the stench and fluids of the body into contact with her skin. Her toes were numb. She clutched the sleeping bag around her shoulders and shivered.

She beat the hatch door one more time with bloodied knuckles. Should she give up and lay in the icy water? Let it steal her breath instead of starving to death as the bones across the room must've?

No one was coming.

Maddie sobbed. "I don't want to go like this." She buried her head in the blanket. Hope and utter despair mingled together in a whirling mix. She screamed again, her throat raw from crying and yelling for hours.

The snap of a branch somewhere nearby stopped her. Her heart throttled into overtime. Was it Dr. Adcock? Had he returned? What should she do? What if he came back to kill her? What if it was someone else? Even if it was him, it was a chance to escape.

Maddie braced her body, ready to leap when the door opened. "I'm down here," she screamed. "Please, open the door." She yelled over and over, the released air raking heaps of coal over her throat. She pounded on the low ceiling. "Please."

She stopped and listened. Silence other than the drip of water. No one answered back. A tree branch must've given under the weight of the rain water.

Maddie collapsed into the corner, all tears dried up from the hours of weeping. Tonight would be her last night on earth. Everything in her body spoke of it.

What of the college degree she'd worked to the point of exhaustion to get? The job lined up to start in July? And Mom? Joze's beautiful hazel eyes flecked with green came to mind. What about Joze? Right when they'd begun to move forward, when their chance had been renewed, she was going to die without him. Alone.

Would this be her tomb? Here, in this bunker of death, she'd draw her last breath. Her head lulled to the side.

What about God? Her chest fluttered. Hadn't Aunt Lonna and Joze told her He loved her no matter what? She had to fight. The only being to hear her was God. The God she'd denied and cursed for too long. Why would He come to her rescue now after all the years of hate? Even He couldn't forgive after all her railing and rebellion. There was no way, was there?

But hadn't Aunt Lonna once said something about people's eternal souls being safe in God's care even when He chose not to protect them from physical harm?

Maddie clenched her shaking hands. Her lips tasted of salt. "Please God, I was so wrong. I don't want to die down here. Please help me. I know I don't deserve anything from You."

With everything she had, Maddie prayed. Peace edged through her heart and began to radiate through her being.

Another snap of a branch and shuffle of leaves made Maddie jump.

47

Joze threw the vehicle into park, grabbed his medical bag and soared out of his car. Rain pelted his face as he stared up at the sky that drew a shade grayer. A whiff of decayed leaves and fresh earth cut him to the bone. He tore up the stone walkway to the Victorian mansion with scrolled woodwork in every corner and against every column along the double-decked porch.

He held his hands in tight fists, the nylon handle of the bag cutting into his right palm, to keep from pushing the doorbell over and over. Water dripped off his nose and ears. Joze ran a shaky hand through his hair and shook off the excess water.

The door squeaked open. The pounding in his chest matched the fast race of water running off an unseen ledge above him. A woman in her seventies held tight to the door for support. He noted the coiffed hair that matched her expensive linen pants and silk shirt almost covered by a wool cardigan. "Hello, ma'am. I'm Joze Evans, and I'm here about a missing person."

The woman blinked hard. "I already talked to the authorities."

He thanked God when she didn't try to close the door before he could explain himself. "I am aware that the state troopers were here, but I had a few extra questions. You are Mrs. Adcock?"

She nodded.

Please don't ask for I.D. Please let the EMT uniform be formal enough. "It's about a woman named Madeline Clare."

"They said my son may've taken that woman." She blanched. "My son did a lot of things wrong, but he wouldn't do something like that. He couldn't."

Joze shook with impatience.

She went on, "You believe he was a stalker? That's what they indicated." She pulled her heavy sweater a little tighter around an average frame and sniffed.

The lights of the huge entryway cast a glow around him. "I know it's hard to accept, but it's a real possibility." She seemed to crumble a little. "I—we have reason to believe Dr. Adcock could've brought her here. Are you sure you haven't seen him or her?" He pulled out his phone to show her a picture he'd snapped of Maddie the night he'd stayed late. "See?"

"They showed me a picture of her, and I'll tell you what I told them. I've never seen her before. My son hasn't been here—" She sucked in air through her nostrils and started to weep. "I can't believe any of this."

He raised his hand. "I understand, but...what if he was here, and you didn't see him?"

She glanced back and then moved out the door and pulled it closed. "I guess it's possible. But why would he bring her here?" She fidgeted with a button on the sweater. "We haven't had a thing to do with him since the trouble."

How much did she know that she wasn't telling the authorities? Was it possible she really didn't have a clue about both of her sons' whereabouts? Better take the heat off the possibility her son had done something horrible before she stopped talking. "Please. Can you think of anywhere he could've gone for privacy here or somewhere else?"

Mrs. Adcock crossed her arms. "No." Her brows furrowed together. "Well, there used to be an old bunker in the forest. We had it built when the Cold War was in full swing. But it was sealed up years ago."

Breathless, Joze put his hands together as if to pray. "Please, tell me where it is." He strained to stay until she answered, ready to make a run for whatever direction she said.

"You think he put that woman down there?" her voice rose, shock evident in her wide eyes. She treaded across the porch and stopped at the corner. "Down the hill and to the left. Let me get the flashlight, and I'll show you where."

He hurdled off the porch. "It can't wait. She could be hurt."

The woman gasped. "I'm so sorry. I never thought..." She hurried back to the door. "I'll meet you down there. There's an old fence post. When you see it, you'll find the bunker straight ahead about fifty feet into the forest."

Joze pulled his phone out and called 9-1-1. Then he ran at full speed down the walk. When the dispatcher answered, he gave the address, stated the emergency, and then hung up, almost dropping the phone on his way past the terraced sections of yard closest to the house.

"Maddie!" He yelled over and over.

Dark shadows closed the tree line in secrecy. He skidded to a stop at the post. His hand slid across the wood, smooth from years of hands touching it. Where,

where, where? "Maddie, I'm coming."

He pulled a small flashlight from his pocket and shined it into the forest. The old leaves from the fall remained encased on the ground, unmoved by the wind of spring. His nerve endings jittered, sending adrenaline through his body.

Straight ahead, he avoided a fallen branch bigger than his thigh, its fresh wound of light wood shredded at its base. No noticeable path led the way. He squinted into the darkness and kept as straight as he could. Ten paces. Twenty more.

The ground was undisturbed. He threw his hands out in frustration. What were the chances she was here if it looked like no one had been in the woods for years? "Maddie." His voice echoed around the trees.

A scuffle and what sounded almost like a whisper caught him off guard. A small mound of leaves marked a change in ground level. "Maddie!"

Her voice carried through the woods as if miles away. Joze rushed to the mound, put the flashlight between his teeth, and then began to shove the leaves away. A graying cement encasement began to show. Thumping met his efforts to clear the top. His hand landed on something long and metal. A crowbar holding the locking mechanism closed. He grabbed the flashlight to get a better look. "I'm here. It's OK."

Maddie belted out a call, "Joze."

He pulled the crowbar out of the loop to a lock and yanked on the cement hatch door. It gave with much grumbling. The unmistakable odor of death reached up and knocked him back a pace.

Maddie tried to climb out of the hole. Joze scooped her up and held tight for a moment before pulling back. "I thought I'd never find you."

She held tight, her eyes darting around the wooded area. "He could come back," she gasped. "It's the doctor. We have to get out of here."

Joze pulled her close again. "He's dead, Maddie."

"Are you sure?" she sobbed.

"Yes. Are you hurt? Any broken bones?"

Maddie scrunched into his grasp, quivering. "No," she spoke through chattering teeth. "Just cold—"

He checked over her body to her wet ankles and feet, the odor slightly coming from her. "Was there water down there?"

She let go long enough for him to pull the thermal plastic blanket from his bag. "The rai-rain was pouring in."

Joze fought the urge to kiss her all over. "It's OK. You're out and safe. And I'm never letting go of you again."

He tucked the blanket around her. Then he took her pulse and checked the blue of her lips. "Think you could make it up the hill? The ambulance is on its way."

Maddie nodded.

He pulled her up. Questions pummeled his thoughts. But now wasn't the time to get answers.

The flash of a light fell on them. Mrs. Adcock held an umbrella in one hand and the flashlight in another. "Miss, I'm so sorry for what my son—" She didn't finish.

Maddie's grasp loosened. "I hate to tell you like this," she still hadn't gotten control of her shivering, "but I think one of your sons is...down there."

The lady's knees seemed to give, and she swayed. Joze had no choice but to release Maddie to catch the woman. "Ma'am, hold on. I've got you."

Shock hit him in the chest like a hammer on an anvil. Maddie had been stuck down there with a dead body for three days? "We'll let the police check it out."

Mrs. Adcock shuddered. "And all this without us even knowing." Her tears returned. "Poor Keith."

Maddie fell against a tree. "You mean Robert."

The lady shook her head but didn't elaborate.

Joze eased her back against another tree. Her skin paled to almost white. He didn't want to injure the woman more with accusations. "I'll explain later."

Voices called down the mountainous slope. Lights recoiled back and forth. "Is anyone down there?"

Joze eyed Mrs. Adcock. "We're here."

He picked up his flashlight and shook it back and forth until the fire and rescue workers thundered to a halt in front of them. He stated Maddie's vitals and condition and then the older woman's, and gave her symptoms of shock.

All the shuffle and noise rebounded off the trees. He went straight to Maddie as soon as a fellow EMT worker took over care of Mrs. Adcock.

One of them stepped in his way. "Dude, I'm not leaving her side." He gave his credentials and the guy moved in front of them to get a look at her. Maddie clenched his hand in hers as they put her on a backboard. He waited for them to strap her in and carry her up the hill.

Her nails almost dug into his palm. "Don't leave me."

"You'll be lucky if I let you out my sight for one second."

She turned up the corner of her mouth.

At the ambulance, Joze climbed in with her. His chest heaved with pent-up stress. How could he tell this woman how much she meant right in the midst of a near death experience?

48

When the doors to the ambulance closed, Maddie shut her eyes for a moment and sucked in a breath. Joze had to know she'd accepted the truth about God. She had to tell him God had been protecting her down in the bunker. She shook off the cloying fear vibrating through her even though she was safe. "God saved me from this, Joze. I know it now."

He pulled back, widened his eyes, and then knelt beside her. "He'll never leave you, even when you think He's far away."

"I get it now. I got things right with Him while I was down there." Maddie tried to turn her head to see him.

He stilled her. "You don't know how glad I am to hear it." The next words he couldn't stop from leaving his mouth. "I love you, Maddie."

She laughed and he jerked his eyes to hers. "I love you too."

His soft lips gingerly touched hers and pushed away the lingering shock. She couldn't move, but there was nowhere else she'd rather be than with Joze.

"Woman, you're mine from here on out...."

She rolled her eyes then laughed. "OK, if you insist."

49

With her diploma in one hand and her other arm wrapped around Joze, Maddie smiled at the camera in her mom's hands. This was a day too long in the making. All her fears and disbelief had been buried in the tomb a month ago. But what about Mom? All the little things Maddie hoped to see change were still the same. Well, except the night Mom rushed to the hospital in Massachusetts where the EMTs had taken Maddie after her rescue. She'd begged forgiveness for her mistakes as a mother and for not believing Maddie. But now?

Maddie shook off the melancholy. Nothing was going to ruin this big day—even the thought that Aunt Lonna wouldn't be there to see her succeed.

Joze tweaked her nose. "What's up?"

With a quick squeeze, Maddie inhaled his enticing cologne and then released him. "You know... Let's pack up and head home."

He followed the trail of her gaze to her mother. "Don't let it get to you. She has to find it on her own."

With a nod, Maddie waved for Mom to join them. Acceptance. That was her new mantra about her mom. "Come on. I can't wait to see my new apartment."

The cousins barreled toward her, Aster in the lead. "Phew, what a long line. How many people graduated with you?"

"Oh, over a thousand." She embraced the two young women. "Thanks for being here." With her hand outstretched, she managed to pat Devin on the shoulder before the pile broke up.

Devin smirked. "Yeah, I wanted to miss it, but..."

She smacked Devin across his bicep. "Ha."

Joze gave him a fake punch in the arm too. "Be nice to my girl."

Her cousin didn't deflect it in time but laughed. "Just kidding."

Where had Mom gone? Maddie checked the emerald lawn where she'd been standing. An ounce of fear pelted her nerves before she could stop the reaction, but then Mom appeared beside her car. Maddie took a deep breath.

Her mother dipped her head and gave a secretive smile. "We have something for you."

"You do? What is it? A nice down payment for my apartment?"

Aster and Jocelyn tittered and joined Mom. "You already got that." She raised the corner of her mouth.

Her cousins helped Sassie pull a thin box wrapped in graduation paper from behind her back, and it wasn't small.

After Maddie tore open the graduation present, she stopped and put her hands to her mouth. A mixture of Aunt Lonna's aromas met her.

"We found this in one of her cabinets. She must've been working on it for your graduation."

How had she missed it in all their searching? Maddie pulled out the handpainted art piece.

"And, I finished it...for her." Mom's mouth pinched together.

A love offering from both. Maddie swallowed

hard. "Thanks, Mom."

She made out the areas Mom had worked on, but they fit beautifully with her aunt's part. Perfect. A treasured gift to remember Aunt Lonna by.

Joze squeezed her shoulders. "Not to take from this moment, but I have something also."

Grasping the present, Maddie turned.

Joze was on one knee. A ring sparkled in his hand.

She put up a finger. "Wait a minute. I thought we agreed you'd pick something more special..." The cousins gasped.

Joze jumped to his feet and sprinted after Maddie as she ran and called over her shoulder, "I'm only joking."

Joze caught her in a bear hug and dipped her. "Take it back."

Giggles kept her from answering.

"Well?" He didn't let her up but tickled her side with a free finger.

"OK, OK," she gasped. "I will marry you." She wrapped her arms tight around him and kissed him for all she was worth.

A Devotional Moment

Each tree is recognized by its own fruit. People do not pick figs from thorn bushes, or grapes from briers. ~ Luke 6:44

Although there are times when people practice deception for a good cause (such as when a law enforcement officer has to go undercover to catch a criminal) many times in life lies cause a lot of damage. We are led to believe one thing, but what we're shown or what we think we know doesn't go with what we feel. Despite what we see, something tells us all is not as it seems. We recognize something is false and must remain cautious. Oftentimes, we're forced to find comfort in the fact that justice will prevail when the truth is finally revealed.

In **Practicing Murder**, the protagonist is stalked by someone who believes she knows about a deception from long ago. Scared and alone, she has to place her trust in a person from her past who lied to her. Despite their history and her hesitation, she must depend on his efforts to discover the truth. Her heart cries for justice, but the evidence points to the wrong conclusion. She is worried that she is attempting to "pick figs from thorn bushes" when her heart chooses to believe he has changed. But the truth will out and love overcomes all.

Have you ever let down your guard and been deceived by someone you thought could be trusted? It's a difficult place to be and makes us wary of trusting anyone else in the future. Have you ever been deceived into thinking ill of someone else, only to find out later that you were lied to and so misjudged an innocent person? This is also a difficult place to be—both as victim and perpetrator. But as Luke tells us, "each tree is recognized by its own fruit", and a person's true colours will eventually shine forth through their own actions and emotions. When you are wronged, don't worry. God will avenge. Forgive. When you've wronged someone else, do what you can to remedy the situation. Then, don't worry. God will extend mercy. In all circumstances, bear good fruit.

LORD, TEACH US TO SEEK TRUTH WITH DILIGENCE. LET OUR HEARTS RECOGNIZE DECEPTION AND SHINE A LIGHT TO REVEAL WHAT WE NEED TO SEE. MAKE US EVER TRUTHFUL AND MAKE US WARY OF THOSE WHO DECEIVE. IN JESUS' NAME WE PRAY, AMEN.

Thank you…

for purchasing this Harbourlight title. For other inspirational stories, please visit our on-line bookstore at www.pelicanbookgroup.com.

For questions or more information, contact us at customer@pelicanbookgroup.com.

Harbourlight Books
The Beacon in Christian Fiction™
an imprint of Pelican Book Group
www.pelicanbookgroup.com

Connect with Us
www.facebook.com/Pelicanbookgroup
www.twitter.com/pelicanbookgrp

To receive news and specials, subscribe to our bulletin
http://pelink.us/bulletin

May God's glory shine through
this inspirational work of fiction.

AMDG

You Can Help!

At Pelican Book Group it is our mission to entertain readers with fiction that uplifts the Gospel. It is our privilege to spend time with you awhile as you read our stories.

We believe you can help us to bring Christ into the lives of people across the globe. And you don't have to open your wallet or even leave your house!

Here are 3 simple things you can do to help us bring illuminating fiction™ to people everywhere.

1) If you enjoyed this book, write a positive review. Post it at online retailers and websites where readers gather. And share your review with us at reviews@pelicanbookgroup.com (this does give us permission to reprint your review in whole or in part.)

2) If you enjoyed this book, recommend it to a friend in person, at a book club or on social media.

3) If you have suggestions on how we can improve or expand our selection, let us know. We value your opinion. Use the contact form on our web site or e-mail us at customer@pelicanbookgroup.com

God Can Help!

Are you in need? The Almighty can do great things for you. Holy is His Name! He has mercy in every generation. He can lift up the lowly and accomplish all things. Reach out today.

Do not fear: I am with you; do not be anxious: I am your God. I will strengthen you, I will help you, I will uphold you with my victorious right hand.
~Isaiah 41:10 (NAB)

We pray daily, and we especially pray for everyone connected to Pelican Book Group—that includes you! If you have a specific need, we welcome the opportunity to pray for you. Share your needs or praise reports at http://pelink.us/pray4us

Free Book Offer

We're looking for booklovers like you to partner with us! Join our team of influencers today and periodically receive free eBooks and exclusive offers.

For more information
Visit http://pelicanbookgroup.com/booklovers